Give Me Thorns

A Lesbian BDSM Romance

ELIZABETH ANDRE

Give Me Thorns
Elizabeth Andre

All rights reserved. No part of this book may be used or reproduced in any manner without written permission of the publisher, except for the purpose of reviews.

All characters and events in this book are fictitious. Any resemblance to actual persons, living or dead, is strictly coincidental.

Other titles by Elizabeth Andre:
The Time Slip Girl
Learning to Kiss Girls
Lesbian Light Reads Volumes 1-6 Boxed Set
The Beauty Queen Called Twice
Skating on Air
Someone Like Her
Taijiku
Joy for Julie
Tested: Sex, love, and friendship in the shadow of HIV

Editor: Cassandra Pierce

A hearty thank you to our beta readers: Liga, Melissa, Robin and Alexandra.

And a special thank you to Vespertine and the Titans of the Midwest.

Copyright © 2016 Elizabeth Andre
All rights reserved.

ISBN-10: 1540510875
ISBN-13: 978-1540510877

tulabellarubypress

GIVE ME THORNS
ELIZABETH ANDRE

The worst day Megan has ever had is about transform her life in ways she never believed possible.

Megan, a long-haired femme lesbian with beautiful pale skin and chestnut brown hair, is having a very loud and public fight with her soon to be ex-girlfriend when a woman on a motorcycle comes to her rescue. Against her better judgement, Megan hops on, and they ride off into the setting sun.

Stevie, a handsome African American butch lesbian with a lock of blonde hair curling out of the front of her helmet, loves rescuing damsels in distress. Sometimes, she just gives them a ride home when they need it. Sometimes she ties them up in her playroom when they are both ready to have some fun.

At first, Megan is terrified of Stevie's playroom, but soon admits that BDSM is something she's always wanted to try. Stevie is initially willing to give Megan a chance but isn't sure about playing as hard as she really wants to with a total newbie.

Together they explore Megan's limits as well as Stevie's and discover that true love requires knowing yourself most of all.

This lesbian BDSM contemporary love story includes numerous scenes of graphic sex and is intended for adults only.

Give Me Thorns

A Lesbian BDSM Romance

ELIZABETH ANDRE

CONTENTS

Chapter One 1
Chapter Two 12
Chapter Three 20
Chapter Four 25
Chapter Five 32
Chapter Six 44
Chapter Seven 52
Chapter Eight 60
Chapter Nine 69
Chapter Ten 79
Chapter Eleven 86
Chapter Twelve 95
Chapter Thirteen 109
Epilogue 120
About Elizabeth Andre 122
Connect with Elizabeth Andre 128

CHAPTER ONE

Megan

There are moments in your life that cannot be planned but change everything. I was about to have one of those moments on a Friday night in the middle of an unusually cool spring.

I was standing in the parking lot of a local restaurant screaming at Paige, my girlfriend, and she was screaming at me. I called her frigid. I begged her to just let me touch her. I said I loved her. She called me sex-obsessed for just wanting to put my hand on her thigh.

I didn't know if I could take much more of this. We had started dating three years ago, and we'd been living together for two. Things had been great until about a year ago when it started to feel like she was pulling away. She was becoming more distant, although I didn't know why. We stopped having sex. I bought sex toys and how-to books and kept trying to pull her toward me, which mostly left me frustrated. I had heard all about lesbian bed death. I always thought it was a myth or at least optional. I wondered if there was something wrong with me. I worried that there was something wrong with her. I loved her.

So, we stood in the parking lot screaming. People may have been staring, but I didn't care. I hadn't had sex in a year, and I desperately needed the touch of another human being. To top it all off, the creepy senior partner at the law firm where I had started working as an accountant a few months ago finally found a reason to have me fired that day. On the way home, I sat on a piece of gum on the bus. When I got home, my credit card company called to tell me one of my cards was being used fraudulently, and I couldn't use it anymore. Yes, I had other cards, but it was my main one. Then my mother called to ask me about how my love life was going.

I really didn't think today could get any worse, and then Paige and I started fighting.

I was ready to break when I heard the dull rumble of a motorcycle pulling up behind me. Paige had just told me that she loved me and wanted to work things out between us. She wanted things to be different, she said.

I then heard the sound of a deep, smooth voice I would grow to love.

"Are you okay?" she asked. "Is this woman bothering you?"

I turned to her with tears running down my cheeks. She straddled a large black motorcycle with legs clad in matching black leather pants and boots. She broke into a smile, revealing subtle lines around her mouth. The whiteness of her teeth and the single lock of blonde hair sticking out from beneath her helmet contrasted with the warm brown of her skin.

I'd never even been on a motorcycle before, but Paige was right about one thing. Things had to be different. Something had to change. We couldn't keep doing the same thing over and over again and expect a different outcome.

"Can you get me out of here?" I asked.

"Where do you want to go?"

I told her I didn't care, and she nodded to the back of her motorcycle. I put my hand on her shoulder and hopped on. She handed me a helmet. I'd never worn one before, but I liked its snugness. As we drove off, I heard Paige yell my name, but I had to get away. There was something about this that was so right, which is interesting because, in comparison to my life up until now, it was so wrong.

I had spent my life making safe, sensible decisions or readily following my parents' decisions for me. In high school, I ran the model United Nations and negotiated enthusiastically for the countries I represented. I got our debate team to the state championships, although we didn't win. I dated occasionally but didn't stay out late and never got drunk. There are no videos on the internet of me going wild because I never did. I got good grades.

When I went off to university in my home state, I chose a school based on a balance between the quality of the program and the financial aid package. I didn't want to be a financial burden to my parents or my future self. I studied hard. I worked hard and landed a plum accounting job right out of school. Some of my fellow students took risks. They traveled the world, occasionally getting themselves or other people into trouble. They started companies that took up a lot of time but didn't seem to really go anywhere. I guessed there was a chance that they would. That's why they did it. They wanted to launch the next Facebook out of their dorm room. I just wanted to get my degree and land a stable job with paychecks that I could always count on. I wanted to meet and fall in love with a woman who would always be there for me. Together we would buy a home with a great lawn and a white picket fence, have kids and live happily ever after.

Being a lesbian was the most out there thing in my life, and it had been enough excitement for me. I hadn't even bought sex toys until recently and only because I hoped it would rekindle the passion in my relationship with Paige.

Tonight, for the first time in my life, I didn't know where I was going, although we were driving into the sunset so I knew we were heading west. I felt a fresh breeze against my skin. The scents of the city changed as fast as the scenery as we drove on. I smelled the flowery sweetness of the newly budding magnolia trees mixing with the smoke-filled exhaust of a car that desperately needed a repair. And all of the scents mixed with the smell of the leather from her jacket. I tried to say a few things, but the woman clearly couldn't hear me over the roar of the motorbike and the other traffic around us. I stared at the back of her helmet. It was matte silver with a little rectangular sticker with black and blue stripes and a red heart. It was cute, although I didn't know what it meant.

My tears stopped falling, and distance started to make me feel better. We pulled into the driveway of a blue Victorian house with a gigantic wrap-around porch. The landscaping was neat but not fancy.

There was no white picket fence.

As she turned off the ignition, she turned to me. "We're here."

Her smile was even more beautiful up close, and I sat there not really knowing what to do.

"Um, you need to get off. Then I can lock up the bike."

I apologized as I pulled myself off and onto the sidewalk. I stood there gripping my purse and wondering what would happen next. I didn't want to go home just yet. Sure, I lived there. It had been my home for the past two years, but it was really Paige's house. She owned most of it, including the white picket fence I'd always dreamed of. I was sure she'd be there. I didn't want to deal with her yet. The neighborhood I had arrived at was purely residential with children's toys in front yards and the occasional budding flower bed. I was pretty sure I could put a hotel room on one of the credit cards I had left, but I didn't see a hotel nearby. I didn't know where I would sleep that night.

The motorcyclist stood in front of me and took off her helmet. She was about my height, and her hair was short, curly and butch. She stood there broad-shouldered and wide-legged like she owned the sidewalk.

"Now what?" she asked with a wry grin.

I gripped my purse closer like a treasured security blanket. At that moment, it was one of the few things in my life that hadn't changed. My bottom lip started to quiver.

"My name is Stevie. How about some tea? Or something stronger?"

I nodded and followed her into what I assumed was her house. The decor was utilitarian with the occasional personal flourish like photos of her with large groups of people. They looked like friends. I had to admit a pang of jealously. I'd done well as a serial monogamist but hadn't had a group of buddies since college.

She took off her black leather jacket, revealing muscular arms and a plain black T-shirt. Maybe it was an indication of how sheltered I'd been, but I could honestly say that I'd never met anyone who looked like Stevie. I followed her into the kitchen. The fridge was decorated with more photos and flags of several kinds. I recognized the rainbow flag and the pink triangle. Another flag with brown stripes and a bear claw was a mystery.

I sat down in a kitchen chair. Make that flopped down. I was exhausted. My life had fallen apart today, and a random stranger, a handsome woman, although not my type, was putting the kettle on for tea.

"What kind of tea would you like?" She opened a cupboard filled with dozens of different kinds. Then she pointed to the top shelf filled with bottles of alcohol. "If you want booze, this is what I got."

I sat there as the kettle approached boiling while Stevie put together a small plate of cookies.

"Thanks, Stevie. I'll take whatever." As the kettle whistled, I realized it was the first time I had said her name. I liked the way it sounded. I'd never met a woman named Stevie before. Maybe that was because I didn't have any butch friends.

It's not like I didn't have any friends. I did have a few, although nothing like the groups of people with whom Stevie seemed to connect. I hung out with co-workers. There was a lesbian dining group I was a member of, but I hadn't gone on any of their outings since I moved in with Paige. I'd kept up with a lesbian book group, although even that had fallen off lately. I had plenty of Facebook friends, but few I saw in real life. I'd been so focused on my career and trying to save my relationship. My closest friend was a gal named Jane. She was a fellow long-haired femme and accountant. We had met in college. Paige must have called her looking for me because she had just sent me a worried text message. I texted Jane back, saying that I was okay and would call her tomorrow.

Stevie had placed the plate of cookies on the table. The sugar cookie covered in chocolate and sprinkled with peppermint looked fantastic. I took a bite.

"This is really good." A few crumbs fell onto the table. I took a napkin from the napkin holder and wiped up the crumbs. I felt my energy starting to return.

"Thanks. A friend made them and dropped them off today. So, Megan, how about some Earl Grey?"

Honestly, Earl Grey was my favorite, and I told her so. I'd just been too upset to articulate that when she asked the first time. She poured the hot water into mugs, and the tea bags released their flavor in brown waves that snaked through the water.

"How do you know my name?" I felt like crying again.

"I heard your girlfriend yell it, and only a girlfriend can trigger that kind of screaming, so that's how I know she was your girlfriend." She sat down opposite me at her kitchen table.

The chair she sat in was a fairly ordinary brown wood with odd metal loops under the arms and behind the legs. *Such an odd flourish*, I thought.

I blew on the tea, trying to get it to cool, but tears were running down my face again. "I don't know if I can go home."

"You can sleep on the sofa. Tomorrow morning you can figure out what to do next." Her voice was gentle with an undercurrent of strength. She wasn't someone to be trifled with.

Now, the tears really started to flow. She handed me a tissue but didn't ask me any more questions. She just sipped at her tea.

"Are you sure? I can go get a hotel room."

She nodded. "It's really late. Just stay here. It's no problem. I have this house to myself. I have a friend coming by tomorrow morning. Actually, she made those cookies you're enjoying. She can take you where you want to go tomorrow." She patted my hand. Her nails were short but neatly manicured. Her hand was so soft. I wondered what she did for a living to have this beautiful house all to herself and such soft hands.

I thanked her for her generosity and her hospitality, but we didn't talk much beyond that. I didn't know what to say, and I had so many thoughts swirling in my head. I was pretty sure I would be able to find a new job, but I dreaded the hunt. I hated not knowing when my next paycheck would come in. And was accounting what I really wanted to do? I wondered if I could go back home tomorrow. Would I be welcome there? Was there any hope for me and Paige?

After we finished the tea and Stevie had cleared away the dishes, she unfolded the sleeper sofa and made the bed with white linens that smelled like they had dried in the sun. I tried to help out as much as I could, but she didn't let me do much more than pull down one corner of the fitted sheet over the mattress while she pulled down the other. She even gave me a toothbrush and a set of pajamas. They were peach with little flowers and didn't look like her style. She said her friend, the same one who had made the cookies, had left them behind.

While she was off getting ready for bed herself, I wondered briefly what she wanted from me or if she would murder me in my sleep. After all, I knew next to nothing about her. Being murdered in my sleep wouldn't be out of line with how bad my day had been already. I sighed and chided myself for the pity party I was kicking off. My self-pity melted away when she came back to check in on me and say goodnight.

She was wearing a white T-shirt and matching boxer shorts that showed off the muscular legs that her leather pants had hidden earlier. She radiated warmth and safety. I saw faded swipes of face cream that she hadn't quite rubbed into her cheeks. I pointed out one smudge that she then tried to ease into her skin but kept missing.

"Here, let me." I got up from the sofa bed and raised my thumb to her face. The lotion didn't smell of flowers like I expected. There was something masculine about it but soft, like her skin, like her. I was close enough that I could feel her warm breath brush my lips. She was close enough to kiss. She was closer than Paige had been to me in months, but I didn't want to think about her. I wanted to think about Stevie. I imagined the flesh that had to be under her T-shirt and boxer shorts. I don't know why I did what I did next. Today was just so crazy. It could have added to the already awkward situation of being a stranger sleeping in her living room, but it didn't.

I kissed her, a light peck on the lips that if pressed I could just say I was saying goodnight to my gracious hostess. She smiled and kissed me back. She wrapped me in her arms and held me. Her arms were strong, but she held me in a gentle embrace.

"Is this okay? I know you've had a truly bad day," she said. "Will you be okay sleeping here?"

It was more than okay. I didn't yet know what she wanted from me, but I didn't care. I needed comfort, and it seemed like she was willing to give it.

"Will you stay with me tonight? I'd really like to be held." That was true. As horny as I had been for months, tonight I just wanted to be in someone's arms.

She nodded, and we got in under the covers. I pushed my back against her front, feeling her breasts against me through her T-shirt, through my pajamas. Once again, she wrapped her arms around me. She became my "big spoon." I became her "little spoon," and slowly I drifted off to sleep.

I awoke to sunlight seeping in through the living room blinds. Stevie was already up. Through my "just woke up" haze, I heard voices—Stevie's and another woman's—coming from the kitchen. I rubbed my eyes, hoping she didn't have a girlfriend. But then, at least for the moment, I had a girlfriend, so I guess it didn't really matter. If this other woman was Stevie's girlfriend, I hoped she wouldn't be mad at me or Stevie. I looked at my phone. There was a message from Jane asking me to call her today, and a message from Paige saying that we needed to talk. *No kidding*, I thought.

I followed the voices of Stevie and the other woman and made my way to the kitchen. The woman, a white woman with long brown hair tied up in a bun, was pouring milk on a bowl of cornflakes in front of Stevie. The coffee pot had just finished percolating. The aroma was deep and rich.

"Do you take milk or sugar in your coffee?" the woman asked. "You look great in my pajamas, by the way. Take a seat."

Stevie greeted me as well. They both seemed happy to see me, which was such a change. I'd had too many mornings where my attempts at light chatter only solicited evasiveness from Paige. I'd forgotten how nice it was to feel like my presence was wanted and not resented.

It occurred to me that maybe Stevie and this woman who could be her girlfriend had an open relationship. I hadn't known any lesbian couples who had been able to pull that off, although Stevie and I hadn't done anything more than a couple of kisses and a cuddle. Maybe she truly was just a friend. If that was the case, it struck me as odd for Stevie to have her pajamas. I pushed those thoughts out of my mind and took a seat. None of that was any of my business. I would go home today. Maybe a night apart had reset my relationship with Paige. We would work things out. She clearly wasn't ready to give up on us, and neither was I.

I focused on the fresh mug of black coffee the woman put in front of me. She said that her name was Kathy and asked me how I was feeling as I added lots of milk and sugar. I liked my coffee pale and sweet, especially in the morning. She asked me if I wanted a bowl of cereal, too. She fussed about the kitchen as Stevie ate and asked how I was doing.

After saying yes to Kathy's offer of cereal, I told Stevie that I was feeling better.

"I'm kind of surprised how well I slept on your sleeper sofa. They're usually not comfortable at all. It could be that I was so exhausted after what went down yesterday." I dug into the cornflakes. With some cold milk, cornflakes were like comfort food to me.

"I'm glad you slept well." Stevie smiled as she brought her coffee mug up to her lips and took a sip. "It's one of the better sleeper sofas out there. I like having people over and if they end up spending the night, there's no reason why they should be tortured."

Kathy's lips curled into a sly and very sexy smile. "Unless to be tortured is *exactly* what they want."

Stevie chuckled, and it was one of the most joyful and sexiest sounds I'd ever heard. It struck me then that the reason why Stevie seemed like such a singular individual to me was the confidence and happiness she radiated. So few people I knew possessed those qualities in tandem, myself included.

I complimented Kathy on her beautiful necklace, a delicate chain joined by a small shiny blue lock that sat snugly against the base of her throat. We talked about shows coming through town, including some ballet companies I really wanted to see, and new restaurants and whether we were interested in trying out adult coloring books. Everyone seemed to be doing them.

Really, I was just dragging my feet. I was very comfortable in Stevie's kitchen, but I knew I had to head home soon. Paige was probably worried about me. I'd been so rash and impulsive last night. It was time for us to really talk to each other.

I got dressed. I offered to launder the pajamas, but Kathy refused. She said she'd take care of them. Kathy and Stevie seemed like sweet people. It was only when I made one final pit stop before heading out that I realized that they were not as sweet as they looked. I don't know how I opened the wrong door while I was looking for the bathroom, but it changed everything.

I opened the door to a room painted black. A black leather multi-level bench with metal clips dominated the center of the room. A dozen paddles and mysterious instruments hung on one wall. A wooden cross hung on another. A cage on a raised platform was in a corner. *So, Stevie hadn't murdered me in my sleep because she'd planned on torturing me in this room. Was that the explanation for Kathy's remark about torture?*

I closed the door as quickly as I could. I had my purse. I was fully dressed. I wasn't interested in dallying anymore. Kathy and Stevie looked slightly bewildered at my haste, but I knew I had to get out of there immediately. I booked to the closest busy street and hailed a taxi. I wanted to get home more than ever. I hoped Paige would forgive me for running off so suddenly.

When I got home, Lulu's car was in the driveway. Lulu was Paige's closest friend. Lulu always seemed to know how to calm Paige down and comfort her. With both of us calmer, we'd have a better chance of talking things through.

I opened the door to the house I had shared with Paige for the past two years. I patted the guardian cat statue in our foyer and walked into the living room. Paige and Lulu were there, and there was indeed a lot of comforting going on. Lulu was on top of Paige, and they were both topless. Paige looked at Lulu the way she used to look at me, with love and desire. They kept kissing fiercely and passionately like I wasn't even there. Each moment felt unreal. Each moment I tried to convince myself that the last moment was my imagination. This was not really happening.

But it was, and it all started to come together. A year ago, Paige and Lulu had gone camping. I had not joined them because camping was not my thing. It was when Paige had returned from the trip that she became more distant. The harder I pursued, the farther away she seemed to become, but I could never get her to explain why. She would usually change the subject when I brought it up.

I stood frozen to the spot. I fantasized about grabbing Paige's prized cheerleader trophy, the one she had won her senior year of college that had sat in the middle of the coffee table for the past two years, and smashing it into Lulu's head. Instead, I just sighed. That was when they realized I was standing there. Paige quickly sat up, which meant Lulu fell off her, knocking over Paige's cheerleader trophy. It didn't break, but Lulu looked bruised. I can't say I felt sorry for her.

Paige stood in front of me scrambling to get her shirt back on. "I can explain."

I stayed silent while she told me that she and Lulu had been having an affair for the past year. They had fallen in love. She didn't want to tell me because she didn't want to hurt me.

"I'm happy with Lulu. Don't you want me to be happy?"

That question got me unstuck, unfrozen. I made a beeline to the bedroom while Paige followed me. She was still talking, but I was no longer listening. I looked at our home like it was the last time I would see it. It certainly was the last time I would ever see it as ours. There was the off-green hallway that we had always talked about repainting but had never gotten around to choosing a color. There was a flyer on the dresser for the ballroom dance lessons that I wanted to sign up for with her. There was the framed photo of us at her sister's wedding. We were smiling and holding hands.

I grabbed my suitcase and threw in as much of my stuff as it could hold. I started to cry again. My life with Paige, the life that had been so good, had come to a sudden end. We couldn't continue as we were, but neither one of us had been willing to move forward until we were forced. Until now.

"I'll come back for the rest of my stuff later!" I dragged the suitcase to my car.

I didn't even care if she heard me. I sat in my car, and the floodgates opened. Sobs wracked my body. I cried until my shirt was soaked, and my head hurt. My nose was full of snot. I made the mistake of looking at myself in the rearview mirror. My makeup was smeared all over my face. I looked like a sad sack clown.

When I looked up, Paige was standing at the giant picture window in the living room staring at me. She waved forlornly. Lulu came up behind her and closed the drapes. I gave the drapes the finger.

I dialed Jane and asked if I could sleep on her sofa for a week or maybe more.

"You're still my friend, right? You haven't installed a dungeon in your house?" She assured me she was my friend, and her house was unchanged. I headed over.

CHAPTER TWO

Stevie

I was just thinking what a lovely thing it was to have two beautiful women with me at breakfast on a Saturday morning when Megan blew through the kitchen and abruptly left as if the house was on fire.

"Wonder what that was about?" Kathy said as she finished clearing the dishes.

"She was pretty upset last night. Maybe it's just more of the same?" I shrugged. Kathy took her place standing next to me, but since Megan was gone it was time for her to get on her knees.

I reached up and yanked on the lock. The metal was cold, but Kathy's alabaster skin was warm. I didn't have to pull hard. Kathy was well trained and had been one of my wenches for nearly five years. She went down and placed her hands behind her back. She stared at the floor. I loved her in this position. The tendrils that had escaped from her bun fell down like gossamer threads around her face.

I had delayed our play date because of Megan, my damsel in distress from last night. I loved damsels in distress, and Megan seemed particularly distressed last night. I was around the corner at the gas station filling up Bud Red, my motorcycle, when I heard her screaming. She was clearly upset and hurting, although it didn't sound like she was in physical danger.

When I arrived, I saw her long chestnut brown hair flailing as she screamed at her beloved. No one screamed at someone they hated like that. If it was hate or indifference, she would have walked away, but she couldn't. It was the scream of someone whose heart was being slowly starved, but who didn't know how to get it fed.

I asked her if she was okay. I was so happy when she decided to get on the back of Bud Red. I hated seeing a beautiful woman that upset. Her deep brown eyes were red and puffy from crying. Her mascara was running down her cheeks. She held me as we rode through the city. She may have been talking, but I couldn't hear her. By the time we got to my house she had stopped crying, but she clutched her purse like it was the last thing she owned in the world.

I took her in because she didn't seem ready to go home. I wasn't even sure she could get herself home safely. She was sober, but so discombobulated. I didn't invite her to stay on my sleeper sofa because I wanted to get in her pants, although I could tell that, even with all her distress, she was a beautiful woman with pale white skin and a dimple just to the right of her mouth. I just wanted to save her. I loved saving women who needed saving.

Call me what you will: a butch, a stud, a leather Daddy. I'm really just a gentle butch who likes rescuing women from terrible situations. I don't like to see women in pain unless they've consented and have clearly said they wanted it. I like dispensing the pain they want so badly, although it's not for everyone. BDSM without consent is abuse. I've been told "no" plenty of times, and I always respect it. Even Kathy sometimes says "no" or uses her safeword when she needs to. That's okay. Sometimes I say "no" too. Some fantasies should not become reality.

I met Kathy while she was in the middle of a run but clearly struggling. Her gait was wobbly. She was moving slowly. She had a desperate look on her face. We've been together happily ever since. She is one of my wenches, but we're not monogamous by any means. She doesn't live with me, although we do spend a lot of time together. She has her own place about a mile away with her three cats. I have a few other wenches. Sometimes they play with each other, and I get to watch.

Megan was lovely to hold last night. She had nice lips and a good, sexy body. That girlfriend of hers sure didn't know how to treat her right. Too many people in this world don't know when they've got something good. Megan was ravenous for the touch of another human being. I hoped she got home safely this morning and that she was okay.

In front of me right now Kathy was at my feet, waiting for me. She was always so patient. I once had her kneel like that for a couple of hours until her thighs shook and she was whimpering. I had told her she wasn't allowed to speak, and she chose to obey.

Kathy has submitted to me, and I have graciously accepted her gift. We don't have a written contract, but we talk a lot, unless she's gagged. We've worked out our rules, but really, we're much like any couple with a fairly healthy relationship. We do a lot of talking.

She was an especially good hostess to Megan this morning, so I gave her the option of making one request for this morning's play date. She wanted the cage. Wonderful! One of my favorites. I told her to get ready and prepare herself. She knew exactly what that meant. She stood up and got naked, folding her clothes neatly in a pile in the corner of the kitchen table. Then she presented me with her collar and cuffs.

I stared at her body, drinking in such a gorgeous sight. I liked doing that before we really got started. It gave me a chance to think about what I wanted to do, to think about what would make us both wet. She had a full bush that I loved to pull on and a beautiful pair of breasts, large and round with perky protruding nipples. I reached up and pinched one and then the other. She sighed gently.

I put on her cuffs and collar and pushed her back down to her knees. The collar was newer, thick black leather with gold metal rings and purple stitching. I had bought it for Kathy for our four-year anniversary a few months ago. The cuffs were older, but still very sturdy with lots of rings that could be clipped in various ways.

One of the nicer things of a well-established relationship is that I didn't have to tell her to follow me to my playroom on her hands and knees. She knew exactly what to do. I smiled when I heard the rings clang against the floor as she crawled behind me. I opened the door to the playroom, and Kathy followed me in.

I was quite proud of this room. I'd bought the house from my aunt who had made her fortune in black hair care products. By playing around in her kitchen, she'd invented an amazing hair cream. A whole line of shampoos, conditioners, creams, and hair oils followed. When she decided she wanted to retire and move to a warmer climate, she asked me if I wanted the house that her hair care products had built. Her kids didn't want it, but it was a good place for me and a good deal. I had made my money through a series of lucky stock deals, and I hadn't needed a job in a few years. I was able to spend my time making this house my home, including creating the playroom I'd always wanted with all my toys well-organized and clean. I did occasionally go out to a local dungeon for some public play and socializing, but it was great to have such a complete set-up at home.

I wanted to hear Kathy scream this morning, so I decided not to use a gag. I slid the latch on the cage and let the door swing open. I motioned for her to climb in so she was facing the wall, and her ass was facing me. She tried to look behind at what I was doing.

"Eyes forward," I barked. She had put in her one request, and I had granted it. Now, she was all mine. The cage was tight, making it nearly impossible for her to move. She could just about manage a little squirming. I loved that. I closed the door, and the metal bars dug into her butt and exposed her asshole to me. I reached forward clipping her wrists to each corner of the cage.

"Do you want to come today?" I put a little more volume and a little more bite into my voice this time. This was my stage, and I loved taking care to get every gesture and vocal inflection just right for maximum effect. Kathy loved it. I knew she was already wet.

"Yes, please, Sir."

"Good to know." I strolled leisurely around my playroom. I was making her wait. She existed for me, and she loved it. She wouldn't even breathe without my permission. She was completely under my control, and her pleasure and pain were at my whim.

There is something wonderful about a long term BDSM relationship. I knew Kathy's limits, both the spoken and unspoken ones. I also trusted her, and she trusted me. It's not enough for a sub to trust a top. The top also has to trust the bottom to be honest about where her head is and what she needs. I'm not interested in hurting anyone. I just want to provide sensations that cause pleasure.

Kathy pulled against the wrist restraints, which pushed her

luscious ass against the bars of the cage, but she could still move her head and chest up and down. I wanted her more immobilized than that. I grabbed three d-rings from a shelf and clipped them to the top bars of the cage and to the rings on her collar. I made sure she could still breathe, but, other than that, she could barely wriggle. She was a beautiful sight to watch, so I took a seat in the giant leather chair in a corner that was reserved just for me.

"Are you comfortable, girl?" I generally stopped using a wench's name during a scene, all part of the mindplay.

"No, Sir,"

"Excellent. You're an excellent bottom."

"Thank you, Sir."

Bottoms always loved a compliment. I was always happy to give them, and Kathy really did deserve this one.

I stuck my hand in my boxers and moved my fingers to my snatch. The sight of Kathy's bondage and discomfort had made me so wet. She struggled as best she could and moaned and whimpered ever louder. She wanted to come, but she knew that, if she did, the scene would end. She wanted this delicious torment to continue as long as possible. So did I, and she knew better than to come before me. I spread my labial lips and stuck two fingers inside me while my thumb rubbed my clit. I pinched my nipples with my other hand until I was breathing heavily and orgasmic spasms flooded my body.

As I caught my breath, Kathy started to beg. That woman really knew how to turn me on, and I really knew how to torture her. I stood up and took off my boxers, grabbing the harness from a hook on the wall. I was deliberately loud about it, clanging the various connecting rings against the wall.

"Please fuck me, Sir. Please, Sir."

"Okay, but you still can't come."

"Yes, Sir."

Her voice had desperate tinge to it. I knew that the orgasm she was holding back was making her clit ache, but I was still not ready to give her that kind of release. I put in my harness the purple silicone dildo designed for her ass. I wouldn't be touching her snatch for a while, and she couldn't touch it either.

I grabbed a bottle of lube from the fridge. I liked giving my wenches a variety of sensations, so I always had room temperature and cold lube on hand. I squirted it directly into her ass, not warming it with my hands before it went in. Kathy gasped and grunted and kept begging me to fuck her, to let her come. I squirted the lube all over my cock. Kathy strained against the wrist restraints, which just made them dig farther into her flesh. Her tits hung down, her nipples hard and erect. Lovely red marks where the metal bars were pressing into her skin appeared on her ass.

"I'll let you come when I've decided that you've screamed enough." This time, I made my voice take on a dangerous edge.

When the tip of my cock touched the entrance to her asshole, her breath got shallower, and she started to shake. I didn't know how much longer she would be able to hold on. To say I didn't care was too strong a statement. I did care, but her needs weren't that important at this moment. Right now, she was a tight hole for me to fuck, and I did as her moans and grunts got louder and she started to scream like the caged animal she was. I pushed my cock in her ass with a solid thrust. She was pleading with me to let her come, but I wanted to come one more time before she did. I pushed my cock in and out of her ass never pulling out completely. The base of my cock kept hitting my cunt, sending waves of pleasure through my clit.

"Scream, you bitch. Scream, wench, or you don't get to come." I pushed in and out faster until the vibrations moved from the tip of my cock to my clit to my belly. You would think I wouldn't be able to feel much through a silicone dildo, but I could. I could feel Kathy shaking and straining against her restraints and the bars of the cage. I could hear metal hit metal. I could hear Kathy screaming, until yes, she had screamed enough. The vibrations sent another orgasm through my body. I was ready to give Kathy the release for which she was screaming.

I pulled out of her ass and changed to a clean dildo. This one was larger than the one I used in her ass, and it was a pale blue. I ran the tip along the lips of Kathy's pussy. As expected, she was wet, no additional lube required. She let loose one last scream as I slid my cock into her snatch.

"You can come. Come now before I change my mind."

I wouldn't have denied her an orgasm. She had been so good. She knew it, but it sounded good.

"Thank you." She yelled as the spasms of pleasure that she had been holding back were finally unleashed onto every cell of her body. "Thank you, thank you, thank you."

I kept fucking her while her orgasms took away what little intelligible speech she had left. The cage shook. Her breasts swung back and forth. When I pulled out, we were both happy and covered in sweat. I threw the dirty dildos into a barrel. Kathy or one of the other wenches would clean them later. I regarded Kathy, admiring what I had done. Kathy would probably feel that fucking for the next week. She would think of me every time she sat down and felt one of the welts left behind on her ass by the cage's bars, but it was time to get her out. She hadn't used her safeword, but a good top—and I liked to think of myself as a good top—could often sense when to amp things up or back off.

I unhooked her wrists and unlatched the cage. She tumbled out into my arms, and I held her. She was deep in bottom headspace and had completely submitted to me. She wouldn't move without me telling her where to and how far. I loved having that kind of power, but it was also a big responsibility. I always tried to respect that. As we stood there in each other's arms, her breathing slowed down to normal. She nuzzled her nose into my neck and cooed a little. I held her a little tighter, gratified at her show of affection.

I loved a good scene and a good end like this. I kissed her warm, soft lips that had done all that beautiful screaming. Her hair had fallen out of the bun, and I ran my fingers through it.

"How do you feel?" I said.

"I can still feel you inside me." Her voice was low and delicate.

I smiled. I wrapped us both up in robes and grabbed her hand, leading her to the living room. She sat at my feet, cooing and rubbing my leg as we watched TV and ate cookies. I stroked her head, face and shoulders and told her what a beautiful bottom she was. She kept thanking me. After a few episodes of *Orange Is the New Black*, she got up to make our lunch, a pair of ham sandwiches and tomato soup.

As our post-sex high faded, we started talking. We planned our next date and shared news about the other wenches. I would play with April in a couple of days. She was celebrating her recent legal name change. She had been assigned male at birth, but that was not a fit for her. She was meant to be April and female and now all her paperwork would reflect that. We were so happy for her. Britney was on vacation this week with her vanilla girlfriend. We didn't play that often, but she was fun. She wasn't cheating on her girlfriend, and I wasn't interested in being anyone's mistress. Rather, they had an agreement that the sexual proclivities the girlfriend couldn't fulfill would be taken care of by me. Emily was taking a little break from playing with us to try out so-called "normal" dating. She said she would call when she was ready.

"Is it time for a new wench?" Kathy bit into another cookie.

I thought about Megan. I remembered how her long hair felt against my skin, and the thought made me smile. More than that, I remembered the need I sensed in her. I wondered if the need was only because she clearly hadn't been touched by her girlfriend in a while. I wondered if she'd ever had rough sex, or at least rougher than I assumed she'd been having. I wondered if she'd be game for rougher fare.

"Megan is beautiful, isn't she?" I finally said.

Kathy just nodded.

CHAPTER THREE

Megan

A few days had passed since my giant blow-out with Paige. She kept trying to get me to talk to her. In several text messages and emails, she begged for forgiveness. She wanted to be friends. She wanted me to understand where she was coming from. *Blech*. I'm not opposed to being friends with exes. I just wasn't even remotely ready for that, and besides, I had more pressing issues to take care of, like finding a new job and a place to live. And my heart was bruised and bleeding. I couldn't drink coffee like nothing had happened with the person who had hurt me. I was crying myself to sleep every night on Jane's sleeper sofa and waking up with red, puffy eyes. I needed eye drops and cucumber slices to look halfway presentable. I knew I could stay with Jane for a while. She was a great friend, but I would need to move on sooner rather than later. We were developing a routine, but I didn't want to sleep on her sofa forever. I couldn't help but notice that it was less comfortable than Stevie's.

Today was actually turning out to be a pretty good day. I was slowly recovering from what I now referred to just as "that day." My new credit card arrived. I gave up on trying to get the gum out of my trousers and threw them out. I ran across some good job leads. I even had a nice conversation with my mother. I thought about Stevie occasionally and how her arms felt so strong around me. I'd never been with a butch woman before, but Stevie made me understand the appeal. There was a strength and male energy mixed with female that seemed so wonderfully complex. I was glad, however, that I got away while the getting was still good. She had at least one girlfriend and what may have been a dungeon. They seemed like nice people, but I wasn't sure I wanted to be a part of that.

I did not want to be tortured on her sleeper sofa, no matter how comfortable it was.

I was at the grocery store getting a few things for dinner when the woman in front of me turned around and smiled. I recognized her necklace with the blue lock before I recognized her face. It was Kathy. Her hair was no longer in a bun. It fell down around her face.

"Hey, are you feeling better?" she asked.

"Um, yeah." I was flooded with emotions. I had met Kathy the day my life fell apart, and that dungeon had freaked me out. A tear rolled down my cheek.

"I'm so sorry, Megan. I know we met under awful circumstances," she said as she paid. "Do you need a hug?"

I stuttered as my groceries rolled along the conveyor belt. "Let me pay for these first."

She seemed so nice and sincere, but as we walked away from the register, I blurted out, "I'm sorry I slept with Stevie, but what were you going to do to me? Is that how you two find victims? She drives around looking for distressed women for you to torture?"

Kathy looked confused and concerned as she fingered the lock around her neck and cocked her head. "You don't need to apologize. We're not monogamous, but I've never tortured anyone without their permission. Otherwise, I'm not sure what you're talking about."

"I found that horrible room. I opened the wrong door." And then it all came together for me. Maybe I had it all wrong? Maybe Kathy was being enslaved and tortured by Stevie? That lock now looked less like a pretty necklace. It looked more like a restraint. Maybe I needed to save her?

She smiled and seemed to be on the verge of giggling. "We really need to talk."

Curious about what she would say, I followed her to the little café in the grocery store and took a seat at one of the tables. I wiped the tear from my cheek and thought about how I could save Kathy. What kind of hold did Stevie have over her? Maybe Kathy was one of those battered women who didn't feel good enough for something better? Maybe Stevie would threaten to out her every time she tried to leave? She couldn't stay with me and Jane, but we could go to the police. They would get her into a shelter.

"So, you found Stevie's playroom, huh? Dark room with lots of toys." She had a knowing look on her face. If I weren't mistaken, she looked satisfied, but about or with what I'd no idea.

This seemed odd. If my theory was correct that she was being tortured in that horrible room, she wouldn't look so satisfied at the mention of it. I looked closely at her face. I didn't see any bruises. I didn't even see heavy foundation suggesting a covered-up bruise or other mark. I did see light brown eyes, full red lips and long lashes. She was pretty. She could have had any woman. She didn't have to be with Stevie.

I nodded. I was still feeling pretty raw from the recent breakup and "that day," but I had to admit it was nice to sit with someone besides Jane. When you have a breakup, you really regret neglecting your friend relationships. I had Jane, but I had only just begun to rebuild my life. And I no longer had work to escape to either. My world felt very small.

"I want you to understand. We weren't going to do anything to you," Kathy continued. "No one goes into that room unless they want to. They certainly don't go in without Stevie's permission. It's *her* room. I'm sure you've noticed that she likes damsels in distress. She does like rescuing, but most of the time that's all it is. It doesn't lead to much more."

"Do you feel safe with her?"

"Of course. I never feel safer than when I'm in that room with Stevie. I love what she does to me. I love what we do together. It's not punishment, at least not in the way you seem to think it is. It's about sensation and pleasure."

I sat in silence, trying to process what she had told me. This was the first time I had ever met anyone I knew to be in a BDSM relationship. I'd heard of those sorts of relationships before, but it wasn't something I had ever considered. I guess that made me vanilla. I'd led a pretty vanilla life, which was my choice. Now here was

Kathy sitting across from me, living proof that I could choose something different, if I wanted to.

"It's a lot to think about, I know. But if you have any questions, don't hesitate to ask." She was really a warm person. I could see why Stevie liked her. Then she told me the story of how they met.

About five years earlier, Kathy had been training for a marathon. She wasn't sure how, but she got lost and disoriented about 20 miles into a training run. Stevie rode up on her motorcycle while Kathy was limping by the side of the road. Kathy climbed on the back and went home with her. Their relationship built slowly from there. It started with water and cookies that afternoon to help Kathy recover from her run. Then they ran into each other at a local dungeon and played. The fact that there was a local dungeon was news to me. Kathy then spent an intense week with Stevie.

"For anyone she's going to play with regularly, she insists on what she calls a 'one-week intensive' just to really get to know each other and be with each other. You live with her, and you're a full-time sub. You really come out of the week wonderfully changed."

I didn't really understand how being tied up and spanked could change a person. I asked her about the lock around her neck. Stevie had given it to Kathy a couple of years ago, and, no, she did not have the key.

"It's not especially strong. I could probably snip it off with some wire clippers from the dollar store. I choose to wear it every day. I choose to be with Stevie."

"Don't you ever want a traditional relationship? You know, with romance and roses and moonlight?"

A wistful look came over her face. "We have romance and moonlight. Stevie even buys me roses from time to time. I love the soft petals, but I also love the thorns. They have a beauty that people don't often appreciate."

They really had a relationship unlike any I had ever had or even heard about. I had to admit that, despite the blue lock, Kathy seemed free. The blue lock, along with everything Kathy told me, made me more and more curious about Stevie. Kathy's life seemed interesting. I asked her a question that had been on the tip of my tongue for the past several minutes.

I leaned forward and kept my voice low. "Why do you like that kind of sex?"

She shrugged. "I really don't know. I just do."

Not the most satisfying answer, but I'd have to be content with it. "What about jealousy? You said you and Stevie both have other women. Isn't jealousy an issue?"

"No. I like the independence I have in my relationship with Stevie. Stevie likes rescuing women in need, but she also likes the women she rescues to stand on their own two feet, you know?" She paused. "Look, you seem very nice. Have dinner with me and Stevie some evening. We can always use more friends, and we'd be happy to answer more questions. Bring your roommate. It'll be fun."

I said yes because I figured why not? I did have more questions and having dinner with Stevie and Kathy would be a great way to get answers. We made plans to have dinner the following Friday. Later, I told Jane that the weird people I had met with the dungeon had invited us out to dinner.

"Oh, and it's not a dungeon. It's a playroom," I said.

"There's a difference?" Jane looked skeptical.

That night, I did something I hadn't done since those lonely nights in my dorm room waiting for some girl to call. I pulled out a couple of my belts and lay down on my bed. I cinched one belt around my waist feeling the leather dig into my flesh and restrict my breathing. I wrapped another belt around my wrists tying them together. I strained against the makeshift restraints and reached my hands down to my snatch. I was wet, and I rubbed my clit until I came.

I stopped indulging in that little bit of masturbatory bondage when some girl finally did call. I never shared my little secret with Paige or any of my other girlfriends. I was afraid they would think I was a freak. After all, I thought I was a freak. I didn't think I could do that and have the nice life I always wanted. I was reminded how good it made me feel. Yes, Stevie's playroom had initially terrified me. Now, I was intrigued. Maybe I wouldn't have to keep my secret much longer.

CHAPTER FOUR

Stevie

I was going out to dinner with Kathy, Megan and Megan's roommate tonight, but first I had something to celebrate with April.

I had first met April a few years ago at the local lesbian bar. It was the place's last night because someone had bought the building to tear down for condos, so our town would no longer have a full-time lesbian bar. Everyone was sad, toasting the old bartenders and sharing fond memories.

Truthfully, it wasn't a great place. I'm pretty sure the expensive vodka had been swapped out for cheaper stuff. It never tasted right, and the music sucked. The dancing was even worse. The wood paneling was reminiscent of a 1970s basement rec room. The bartenders were never that friendly. But it was for us. It was ours.

When I first saw April, she was sitting at the bar. There was something different about how she moved. Her long blonde hair fell over her face. She looked so forlorn and kept staring at her hands.

My tendency to want to save damsels in distress kicked in. I walked over to where she was sitting and offered to buy her a drink.

"Hey, don't be so sad. We'll find other places to hang out."

"No, that's not it." She ordered a whiskey sour.

I gave her shoulder a friendly nudge with my shoulder. She could barely muster a smile but did manage to flash me a beautiful pair of pale blue eyes. She looked like she was on the verge of tears. I brushed a stray hair out of her eyes and noticed that her hands were large, her shoulders broad. She had an Adam's apple, but I didn't care.

Some people were really picky about wanting the women in their lives to be born women and stay women. I wanted my women to be women when I was with them. I didn't care if they grew up as boys. I'd had one partner become a man. We were still friends, although not lovers. He was fond of saying that transmen were not lesbians. I never disagreed, and I never understood why he kept repeating that. Maybe it was for his own benefit. In any case, I never stopped loving him, but I lost interest in him sexually. He may have no longer been a lesbian, but I still was. He moved to another city and was happily married with a couple of kids. I get a Christmas card from him every year.

But back to April.

She talked about coming out at work that day as transgender. She still had her job, but she wasn't sure how long it would last. Her wife was having second thoughts about their marriage.

"I thought coming out would make things better. I thought transitioning would change everything. It did change everything, just not in the way I thought it would." She chuckled, ruefully. "But look at my hands. They are always going to look like man hands."

I told her that her hands looked strong and beautiful. I complimented her manicure and her silver bracelet that clanged against the bar, but mostly I listened and introduced her to some people I knew. It was a shame it would be our last night together, but you never knew where an introduction would lead.

We didn't have sex that night, but we did exchange contact details. She didn't need a lover that night. She needed a friend. I thought she deserved one. She'd lost a lot by transitioning. The changes in her body were much desired, but scary, and not quite enough. Change always involves loss even when it's the right thing for everyone involved. When her divorce was finalized, we celebrated at one of the gay-ish bars that were becoming more common. Bars exclusively for gay men or lesbians were disappearing. Everyone and anyone was welcome to spend their money at this place, even straight people.

That night I spanked her for the first time. At her request and my desire, I used my bare hands and my favorite wood paddle to turn her ass bright red. After that, we started playing on a regular basis.

This afternoon we would celebrate her legal name change. Her old identity would disappear, and she would fully be the April I had always known.

When she arrived, she proudly showed me her new driver's license, pointing to where it said, "April" and "female." I popped open a bottle of champagne. I'd never seen her so happy. I wondered if I could make her even happier.

"You've worked hard for this." I raised a champagne flute to her. "Wanna play?"

Her grin got a little bigger.

"I'd like to tie you up and fuck you hard."

My relationship with Kathy was so well established that we didn't have to discuss much. We'd already done so much negotiation. Since I didn't play with April that often, we had to do more talking. She wanted to pick out the dildo I would use. We reminded each other of our safewords. I told her that I would check in with her periodically, and she was to honestly tell me whether things were green, yellow or red or, in other words, go, slow down or stop. I wanted to restrain her to my sawhorse and touch every inch of her beautiful body. She agreed.

I told her to get ready and wait for me by my playroom door. She knew better than to go in without my permission. I went to my bedroom to get dressed in my leathers. They seemed appropriate for this scene, and I always liked any excuse to wear them. I took off my cotton T-shirt and bra and put on a black leather vest. The thick leather brushed against my bare nipples making them hard. I took off my jeans and underwear and replaced them with a dildo harness and my leather pants. I grabbed my packy, a brown flaccid fake penis that I used to give myself a bulge and stuffed it into my crotch. My black leather boots with hard heels that made a satisfyingly clomp every time they hit the floor completed the outfit.

When I walked over to my playroom, April was standing naked just outside the door. Her hands were behind her back, and her eyes were down, although I saw her smile as I approached. She had already put her wrists and ankles in leather cuffs. I pulled on the cuffs to make sure they were good and tight.

"Not bad," I said.

"Thank you, Sir."

I gave her an appraising look. Yes, she still had man hands, but she was consistently getting better at moving her fingers in a more feminine manner. It made her hands seem smaller. Her tits were a perfect pair of b-cups with large nipples that I was looking forward to playing with. She got to design her breasts herself. Might as well go for the best you can get.

I stroked the scar on her belly. I knew that was from a suicide attempt a long time ago. We didn't talk about that, but I always liked to show that part of her body some love. So much of her pain was trapped in that spot. Her penis and balls hung down, although we didn't really talk about that either. We agreed that they didn't really exist. April was unsure about surgery to change her genitals, but I found them easy to ignore. I would support whatever she decided.

I, however, didn't want my cock and balls ignored. I was ready to play. I latched my finger into a metal ring on her collar as I opened the playroom. The delicious scent of leather and wood hit my nose. I pulled her down to her knees, and we entered the room with her crawling behind me. She moved over to the shelf of clean dildos. I watched her pick out a red one with corkscrew ridges. She crawled back toward me, carrying the dildo in her teeth. I wondered what she would look like sucking on it when it was in my harness, but I knew I wouldn't have to wonder for long. She got up on her knees and unzipped my pants. My little packy peeked out.

She nuzzled her nose in my fly. I was getting wetter. I ran my fingers through her soft hair and my fingers along her ears as she started to lick the tip of my flaccid silicone cock. My clit became erect as she slipped my packy out of my pants and replaced it with the hard dildo. The harness kept my red dick firmly against my pussy as she gave me a blow job. She ran her tongue up and down my shaft, periodically taking almost all of my cock into her mouth. When her mouth was full, she looked up at me with those lovely, happy eyes. I signaled her to keep going. I wanted to come first before I fucked her.

"Keep sucking." My voice was low and deep. "I'll fuck you after I come."

She resumed licking, covering my red cock with her saliva. The base kept pushing against my clit, sending waves of pleasure through my body, and she kept sucking. She was so hungry. When I fucked her, she was always a woman in my eyes. I hoped she felt like a woman then. Today, she was legally a woman, and she was more eager than ever.

She pulled away from my cock for a moment. "I want to please you," she said.

"Just keep sucking." My body started to shake almost as soon as she resumed sucking. The orgasm ran through my body like a sigh. Now I was ready to fuck her.

I tapped her on the head to stop and ordered her to get on the horse. She scrambled on top of the leather covered contraption. I attached her to it so all she could do was struggle. Her head hung down off the edge of the horse. I clipped her collar to an attached ring so it would stay that way. Her arms and legs rested on pads on the contraption's sides. I bound her wrists and ankles to the horse with small but strong d-rings. Her breasts were on either side of the center bar of the horse.

I pushed her hair aside and blew into her ear, making her gasp and squirmed.

"Are you comfortable?" I whispered.

"No, Sir," was her breathy reply.

"Good. How do you feel? Ready to get fucked?"

"Green. Yes, I am."

"Good to know." I would fuck her in her lovely creamy ass that was wide open for me, but not yet. I would torment her first.

I ran my finger down the center of her back, which caused her to start breathing heavily. I will confess I paused for a moment where the crack of her ass began. I wondered what Megan would look like strapped to my horse. What would it be like to have her under my control? Was she as vanilla as she seemed, or would she let me spank her ass like April was letting me do now?

I raised my hand and quickly lowered it on April's wriggling ass. I paused for another moment to watch the red mark I'd made fade away. Then I lowered my hand again, faster and harder.

"Thank you, Sir," she said as I brought my hand down on one ass cheek and then the other. The red marks were lasting longer. I glanced over at my toy wall. I chose the maple wood paddle with the word "Mine" engraved it. I presented it to her lips, allowing her to kiss it before I once again started working on her ass. Every time the paddle landed, the word "Mine" appeared in her flesh. She was mine this afternoon. I was honored to accept the gift of her mind and body.

When her ass was radiating heat, I traced my finger around her asshole.

"Are you ready for me?"

"Oh, yes, Sir. Green."

"No." I loved teasing her. She pulled against the restraints. I double-checked them to make sure they were tight and cutting slightly into her skin. Then I went to her breasts.

I grabbed a pair of nipple clamps. I fastened one clamp to her right nipple, ran the chain they were attached to under the center beam of the sawhorse, and attached the remaining clamp to her left nipple. I yanked on the chain a few times making her squeal. Every time she bucked, she pulled her own nipples. It was such a beautiful sight to see. She could barely move. What little movement she did have caused her painful pleasure. I removed the clamps for just a moment letting the blood flow back in. Then I put the clamps back on. I took the clamps off and on a few more times. I knew from what April and my other bottoms had told me that each time was more intense.

"What will you do to get me to fuck you?" I asked.

"Anything, Sir. Anything, Sir. Please."

I strolled to the shelf to get my lube. I knew April liked the room temperature stuff, and today was such a special day for her. I lubed up my cock and her asshole until we were both wet and slippery.

"Struggle more." I knew that every time she moved, she pulled on her nipples. The leather restraints would pull on her neck, wrists and ankles, but she obliged. I tapped her sore, red butt cheeks with my cock, and she kept begging.

"Please, I want you inside me, Sir. I need you inside me. Please, Sir."

I could have watched her struggle all day. I could have denied her orgasm for the rest of the day. I could have left her bound all night while I went out to dinner. We had actually done all of those things at least once in the past. Fond memories, and, today, I would fuck her, and she would come. I slipped the head of my penis into her ass. April's breathing became shallow and ragged. I pushed in my dick as far as it would go. She had become a lovely hole for me to fuck, but I could not forget what a special day it was. I needed to say it loud and clear.

"Woman, you may come."

"Oh, thank you, Sir."

I kept fucking her hole as great spasms wracked her body. She grunted, moaned and squealed. I ran my hands over every inch of her body that I could reach. The rings that held her fast clanged against the sawhorse. Her hair flopped back and forth. She yelled for God.

I plunged in one last time just as what looked like her last orgasm ran through her body. I pulled out slowly, and everything in her let go. Her breathing slowed down. She thanked me over and over.

I threw the dildo in the barrel with the rest of the dirty ones and got to work getting April off the sawhorse. She bit her lip and let loose a little sigh when the nipple clamps were released. I unclipped her neck, wrists and ankles, and she rolled off the sawhorse into my arms. I wiped her eyes and mouth with a towel. I checked in with how she was feeling. She said she'd never been happier.

I spent the rest of the afternoon with her, feeding her cookies and watching reruns of *Judge Judy*. I told April about Megan. She said it sounded like I liked her.

I turned down the volume on the TV a bit. "She is beautiful, but I don't even know her, at least not yet. I know so little about her. She presents herself as so respectable, you know. Like nothing's ever out of place. She may not even be into this kind of stuff, and I don't do vanilla sex."

CHAPTER FIVE

Megan

I liked the fact that Kathy and Stevie arrived on time at the Italian restaurant we had chosen for dinner. Mama's Italian Cooking, a restaurant I'd been to many times before, had good hearty bread and pasta. Good comfort food and a familiar setting to meet and learn about unfamiliar people.

We were seated at a booth at the back of the restaurant. I sat across from Stevie, and the table's candlelight cast dramatic shadows across her face. The candles' reflection flickered in her dark brown eyes. Her nose was flat and broad, her skin supple, although there was a tiny scar on her chin. Kathy sat next to her. Today her hair was down. It looked like it had been straightened, and she wore a little makeup.

They were both so sexy, but in such different ways. Kathy had a wholesome look about her. Her face had an appealing warmth that made her seem approachable. The blue lock she wore around her neck, now that I knew what it meant, did nothing to detract from that freshness. Stevie exuded a quiet yet unmistakable strength. When she smiled, which she didn't do as readily as Kathy, it was as if a sunnier part of her disposition had been switched on.

We talked about where lesbians hung out since the closure of the town's last lesbian bar and the wacky weather we had been having lately. We'd had random hail last June and sunny days in December. I talked about my nascent job hunt, and Jane talked about possibly getting a dog from the local shelter.

"I really do think it's time for me to take care of more than a plant," she said.

Kathy, who was the periodicals librarian at a local university, entertained us with stories of some of the wackier things that had been found in the book drop. "One winter an entire family of raccoons just moved in for the night. They did not appreciate getting woken up in the morning."

I learned that Stevie had an MBA. That surprised me, although I guessed MBAs didn't wear suits all the time. She said she'd gotten an MBA for the networking opportunities more than anything else.

"There really wasn't anything in the curriculum that enhanced anything I didn't already know. It confirmed what I already had learned by working with my aunt." She explained that her aunt had made a lot of money selling the hair care products she had developed. Stevie had started working for her aunt when she was still in high school. "I did just about everything in that company. Packaging, delivery, marketing and promotion, bookkeeping, ordering, inventory, secretarial stuff. You name it. My aunt made me learn shorthand, for Pete's sake. The best business education I could have ever had, without question."

After her MBA, she decided to apply her business skills in a different way and became a stock market trader. Her own investments had paid off so well that she didn't have to work anymore, although she did manage her money so it worked for her. That surprised me, too. She didn't look wealthy, but I didn't really know what wealthy looked like. I thought it meant expensive things.

"I have my home. I have my motorcycle. I have enough." She picked up a breadstick, broke it in half and gave one half to Kathy.

"What about that room?" I wanted to move things toward learning more about "that room."

Before Stevie could answer Jane asked her to pass the pepper and started talking about the three-mile run she took this morning.

"I started running regularly about three months ago. I'm really starting to love it. And that's how I justify this pasta alfredo. It's so good."

Kathy gave me a wink, although I wasn't sure what she was trying to communicate. I had no doubt that she must have told Stevie about our conversation at the grocery store a few days before. Instead of steering this conversation back to "that room," Kathy started talking about how delicious her angel hair pasta with artichokes and black olives was and how good her own three-mile run that morning had been. I went along briefly with the conversational detour and said my lasagna was lovely. I had nothing to contribute regarding working out because my life was still off-kilter, so exercise was the last thing on my mind.

Kathy kept Jane's attention while Stevie ignored the conversational detour, although she played coy. "What room do you mean? Laundry room? My walk-in closet?"

I could tell she was teasing me, but I wasn't put off. "It's the one you have on the first floor, that's all black, with the leather and the paddles and the cage."

Reassured that I was not in danger of being chained into that room against my will, my curiosity was piqued. Kathy and Stevie were unlike any people I had ever met. They acted like girlfriends and clearly loved each other, but they didn't live together. They weren't monogamous. They didn't seem to have a problem with jealousy. Kathy was so sweet and unassuming, even though I knew she had been in that room with Stevie many times and said it had been fun.

Jane finally gave up on changing the subject to something tame and asked Kathy, "What does that lock mean?"

"It means I choose to belong to Stevie." Kathy smiled serenely and twirled pasta around her fork.

"So, you're a slave?" Jane's tone was tart, sardonic.

Stevie rolled her eyes and put down her fork, as if in exasperation. "Nah, I'm much more creative than that, and my ancestors were slaves. I'm not interested in owning anyone. She's my wench. Doesn't she look pretty?"

I nodded. "She really does." It felt weird to compliment the looks of someone else's girlfriend who was being shown off like a new car, but they both seemed so charming and happy. I wanted to know so much more. "Will you show me your playroom? I'd like to see it when I'm not freaked out."

"I'm sorry you saw it that first time," Stevie said. "You weren't supposed to."

Jane put her hand on mine, prompting me to remember she was there. I had become so focused on Stevie that I'd forgotten about Jane and my food.

"I'm not sorry." I said.

Jane cleared her throat and tried to speak low and through nearly closed lips so Stevie and Kathy wouldn't hear. "Remember how you asked me to join you to keep you safe?"

Jane pulled me out of the booth. We nearly collided with the server who had arrived to clear the dinner plates.

"Excuse us. We'll be right back. Just need to dash to the ladies." Jane kept a tight grip on my hand. Kathy raised an eyebrow but gave us a little wave as we disappeared.

"What do you think you're doing?" Jane spoke in a low but agitated whisper as she rushed me to a corner of the ladies room. "Why am I even here?"

It took me a while to figure out what to say because I wasn't entirely sure what I was doing. I certainly didn't want Jane to think I was a freak. Yes, Stevie's playroom scared me at first, but now I was intrigued. I was attracted to Stevie when I first saw her primarily because she rescued me. Now I was starting to think I wanted more than a hero. I was starting to think that I, like Kathy, wanted some thorns.

"My life is changing, Jane. I don't know what it's changing to. I do know I want to do things differently. Maybe I've been too safe in my life. But I need you here to support me. I need you to be my friend."

She hugged me. "I don't know what I'm supporting here, but I always have your back. Promise."

When we got back to our booth, Stevie and Kathy were perusing the dessert menu and debating cannoli versus cheesecake but eventually decided on the lemon meringue. Jane and I decided to share a slice of tiramisu.

We ate dessert while discussing the more banal topics of the evening. How had global climate change recently affected the supplies of tomatoes at the local grocery store? Would the host city for the Summer Olympics be ready in time? What was up with a certain lesbian celebrity? It seemed like she'd gained a lot of weight.

"She's gotten so old!" Jane plunged her fork into the tiramisu's brown cream. "And I used to have such a crush on her."

"Guess aging happens to everyone. Oooh, this meringue is good," Kathy said.

There was something about losing nearly everything and still standing that was really giving me courage. And I felt like an opportunity was slipping away. I wasn't about to let that happen.

"I'm not sorry that I saw that room. I'd like to see it again." I licked some of the tiramisu cream off my upper lip and set my fork down with a decisive clunk.

Jane gave me a sideward glance, but let Kathy distract her with her own celebrity gossip.

Stevie smiled, and her eyes seemed to acquire a subtle glow. "How about tonight? After dinner? You free?"

I realized that I was free. "Sounds great." I suspected Jane may have just managed to stop herself from rolling her eyes.

Kathy said she wouldn't be there tonight. "Working tomorrow. You guys have fun."

Stevie would take Kathy home after dinner. I would take Jane home, and then head to Stevie's place.

"What? I don't get to see this infamous dungeon… Oh, excuse me, playroom." This time she did let her eyes roll, and her voice was in full sneer.

I was ready to top her sneer with some heavy sarcasm. "Seriously?"

"No, not seriously, just take me home after dinner, and you can go off and have some fun. Why am I here again?"

Kathy looked directly at Jane, hitting her with those fabulously intense blue eyes of hers. "I've really enjoyed meeting you. I'm glad you're here."

Jane smiled and blushed a little before returning her attention to the tiramisu. After paying up, I took Jane home.

"Are you sure you want to do this?" Jane asked as I pulled up in front of her apartment complex. "You haven't even recovered from your breakup with Paige. And you still have to find a job. They were really nice enough, but…"

"I'm just going to see the playroom. I'm not marrying her."

I understood why Jane was concerned, and it wasn't just because of who Stevie and Kathy were. I had a history of moving too fast, so did Jane, although she had been single by choice for more than six months. It was just a few days ago that I was weeping in her arms and eating all of her chocolate ice cream. Three years ago, just before I met Paige, I was crying over Jill, and, yes, Jane had comforted me. I'd done my fair share of comforting Jane when she needed it after a breakup. She just tended to take longer breaks between break ups.

"If I don't hear from you by noon tomorrow, I'm calling the police." She got out of the car and then leaned in before closing the door. "You don't know these people. *None* of our friends know them. They seem nice, but be careful. You know, being single for a while would not be the worst thing that ever happened to you."

I told her not to worry. As I drove over to Stevie's I started having second thoughts, though. I had said I just wanted to see the playroom, but I was pretty sure I wanted more than that. What if Stevie didn't? If what I really wanted was in Stevie's playroom, what did that say about who I was as a person?

I pulled into Stevie's driveway and sat for a moment. The neighborhood looked so normal. The house looked like any other house on the block, but I had seen that room. I knew it wasn't just another house. I took a couple of deep breaths. I heard her motorcycle pull into her driveway. I was a little shocked that the mere sound of her motorcycle turned me on. I felt some squishiness in my panties.

Stevie waved. "Come on in anytime."

I watched her walk up the front walk, up the steps to the porch and into her house. She was spectacular, her all in her leathers. I never thought I could actually drool at the sight of another human being, but I felt a little trickle of moisture at the left corner of my mouth. More deep breaths. I ran my hand across my mouth to wipe it. I could have pulled out of her driveway and gone home then. I could have spent the rest of the evening looking at job listings and personal ads, but then I remembered what it felt like to have my wrists restrained. I'd never met anyone else who even hinted that they may be up for something like that, despite the popularity of *Fifty Shades of Grey*.

As I walked up the stairs to Stevie's house, I noted how ordinary it was. The last time I'd been here, I'd been too upset to take in all the details. One of the window screens had a small hole and a little bit of rust. A few dried-up leaves had not yet been swept away and were scattered around the front porch. The porch swing was creaking in the wind and needed some oil.

The front door opened to a vestibule. Stevie's leather jacket hung on one hook. A denim jacket covered in patches hung on another. A tiny table with a bowl of keys and various tchotchkes sat in a corner. Photos of flowers hung on the white walls. The house still looked as utilitarian as it did on my first visit, but now I was seeing details that I had missed.

The living room where I had slept in Stevie's arms was before me. The sofa, pale green and fabric covered, was folded up ready for people to sit. I looked closer at her photos. In one she was with a bunch of women in leather, including Kathy, in what looked like the gay pride day parade. In another she was with a bunch of big guys with beards, and it looked like a camping trip. In all her photos she was front and center and almost glowing with happiness.

"Thanks for coming over!" She was in the kitchen. "Come on in. I just boiled the water for tea."

She really did have a beautiful voice. It was deep and firm but still clearly female. The kitchen was just as ordinary with fruit-patterned wallpaper and the usual appliances.

"Do you want Earl Grey again?" As she had that night when I slept over, she opened the cabinet with all the tea on the bottom shelf and the alcohol above.

"You remembered."

"Of course." She smiled and set up two mugs.

I felt stupidly grateful that she remembered my drink of choice. I began falling into a pity pit, remembering Paige and how she used to hold me through the night, like Stevie had a week ago. *Snap out of it.*

As we sipped our tea, she told me more about herself, the MBA she had earned from a top business school, the job that was too perfect, the investments that paid off and the ones that didn't.

"I felt the market crashing a few years ago, so I took the money and ran. Then my aunt offered to sell me this house. It was such an irresistible steal between the low price and the tax break I got from buying it. I've set up my money so that I'm comfortable. I'm not a billionaire. I'm comfortable. Very comfortable."

I told her about my life, about becoming an accountant, about falling for Paige, about living with Jane now.

"My life was good, but it just completely fell apart last week. I don't know what I'm going to do."

She put her hand on top of mine. She didn't squeeze or grab. The hand just lay there, radiating warmth. "Well, you don't have to solve everything tonight. What do you want right now, besides tea?"

I looked down at my mug of tea. I'd added a little milk to it. The pale brown liquid was always so reassuring. I got up from the table, left the kitchen, walked down the hallway and stopped outside the door to the playroom. A couple of moments later, Stevie sauntered down the hallway toward me. She was looking a bit cocky but not in a cruel or nasty way. It was charming. She stopped right in front of me, regarding me for a moment with amusement and, I thought, affection.

She opened the door and gestured for me to step inside. "You have my permission."

The playroom was as different as the rest of the house was ordinary. She stood at the doorway as I ran my hand over the leather bench that she said was a sawhorse. I tapped my nails on the cold bars of the cage. I stared at the rack of wooden paddles and floggers and the table of multiple dildos.

"Why so many different kinds?" I asked.

"Because they're fun."

I pulled a metal tool with spikes off the wall. "Is this fun?" I was skeptical. Some of the stuff was attractive. Some of it scared me. This one looked like it could really hurt.

"In the right hands and with the right person, yes. But if you're not into it, then no."

She seemed so calm. I felt a mix of emotions. My fear of her had faded. My desire for her to touch me in a way that no one else ever had was growing. I was afraid to walk away. I was afraid to stay.

I pointed to the leather straps hanging from a hook on the wall. "I sometimes bind my hands with a belt and then rub my clit until I come." Even in this environment I was embarrassed to say that. I'd never told anyone else about it, and I'd only started doing that again recently after so many years of depriving myself of that pleasure. I was saving myself, but I didn't know for what.

"You can try on the cuffs if you like." She pointed out the cuffs.

They were thick and black, far stronger than the belts I'd been playing with. I pulled one cuff tight around my wrist and then the other. They could have been chained together, but they weren't yet.

I held my wrists out for her to see. "How do they look?"

She licked her lips, clicked her tongue. "Delicious."

"What now?" I was more convinced than ever that I wanted to have sex with her. I wanted more than a cuddle.

"Depends." She took a step toward me. "What do you want?"

"I want you to bind me and make me come." She was close enough to me that I could feel her breath on my face. I wanted her to touch me.

She looked doubtful. "You're sure?" She was playing with me already.

"Oh, yes. This is what I want right now."

A brief smile animated her face. "Well, okay, then. I guess you better get naked."

I paused for just a moment before I took off my top. Stevie directed me to fold it in a corner. I felt butterflies in my stomach. I felt like that first time I'd had sex with a girl in my college dorm room. That night would become the first in months that I didn't masturbate, that I didn't bind my wrists. That night with that girl I came in great spasms by someone else's hand.

I was scared then, too, but that night opened the door to do much more.

Then my bra, trousers and underwear came off. As I undressed Stevie gave me a safeword and told me to use it if I needed it. She asked me about the things that turned me on and the things that left me cold. I was attracted to the paddles, but the floggers didn't interest me. I liked the look of the yellow vibrator, but the dildo that looked like a penis turned me off. I told her that this was the first time I had ever done anything like this.

"I'll go slow."

She directed me to put on a pair of ankle cuffs and checked to make sure they were tight. She put her hand at the back of my head. She pulled me closer to her. I kissed her, first lightly, then deeply, like I hadn't kissed anyone in a long time. Again, I remembered Paige, the first time we kissed and the last. We hadn't had passion in so long.

And then I thought of Stevie. She was so beautiful. No, make that handsome. The blond lock of hair at the front of her head bounced as she moved.

I had always wondered why a woman would want to be mannish, but tonight I didn't care. I was glad she was exactly who she was. I had always wondered why a feminine woman, like me, would desire a butch woman like Stevie. Now, I was so attracted to her. I didn't care why. I just knew it to be true. I wanted Stevie.

When she pulled away, she said, "Since it's our first time, I'm going to do a lot of talking. I'll tell you what I'm going to do. I'm going to ask you a lot of questions. I need you to be relentlessly honest. How does that sound?"

I didn't answer at first. I was tongue-tied. This was all so new to me. As odd as it sounds, I'd never been with a lover who was so gentle and caring. I didn't know whether to laugh or cry at that realization.

She backed away. "I mean it. You have to answer every question."

"That sounds good to me," I stuttered out.

She wanted to bind me to a massive wooden x on one wall. She called it a St. Andrew's Cross.

I whispered, "Yes."

She clipped the cuffs on my wrists and ankles to metal rings attached to the cross, and she even showed me how I could unclip myself if need be. My breasts were exposed. I couldn't close my legs, and I was wetter than I ever remembered being.

She put her hand on my snatch. "You want to come?"

I nodded. I didn't trust my voice anymore, but I managed to whisper, "yes" again.

"Nah. It's far too soon." She removed her hand. "I will always listen to what you say, although I won't always do what you ask me to. Sometimes I'll do what I think you need rather than what you say you want. I will always honor your safeword, without negotiation. Do you understand?"

"Yes." I pulled on the cuffs. I knew how to get out of them, but I didn't want to. I liked their snugness. They held me tight. "Yes. I understand."

I relished the feel of Stevie's hand as she moved up from my snatch to my belly. Her fingers circled my belly button, sending sensations down to my clit.

"Since you said that you wanted me to make you come, you can't come until I've given you permission to do so. Agreed?"

"Agreed." My voice was already breathy and ragged.

She grabbed the yellow vibrator and placed it right on my clit. I felt like screaming. I had to bite my lip and clench my teeth to stop myself from coming immediately, but I didn't want this to end. I bucked against the restraints. She removed the vibrator.

"Is it hard not to come?" She stepped back.

"It's so hard." I felt like screaming, but my voice came out in a whisper.

"Do you like this? Speak up."

"Yes!"

She stepped back farther and unzipped her fly. She reached into her own pants to her clit while I struggled unable to touch mine. This was so unfair, and I loved it. The metal rings clanged against the wooden cross, and she rubbed herself until an orgasm ran through her body with sharp jerks and spasms.

"I always get to come first," she said, zipping herself back up.

I writhed as much as I could as she approached me again with the vibrator. She ordered me to kiss it, and I did. It tasted of me and bright yellow plastic. She rubbed her hands over every square inch of my body as I moaned and groaned. I started to beg for the vibrator on my clit. She kept teasing me, briefly touching the vibrator to each of my nipples. At times, I didn't know if it was the hand on my skin or the vibrator or both.

And then the vibrator approached my snatch again. She rolled the vibrator up my thighs until it was just grazing my labial lips.

"Oh, please," I said.

The vibrator stayed on my labial lips another minute longer before she slipped it in and hit my clit. I started to orgasm, but she removed it.

"I didn't say you could come, Megan. Did you forget?"

"I'm sorry." My clit was pulsing and begging for more. "I don't know how to do this. I'm sorry."

"Okay, since it's your first time, you can come."

The vibrator plunged back into my pussy and landed squarely on my clit. I felt the vibrations radiate through to my fingertips and my toes as the orgasm let loose. I grunted, groaned and yelled out Stevie's name. She pulled the vibrator away, giving me a break for only a few seconds before she reapplied it. This time the orgasm was even stronger and ran through me until I begged her to stop.

Her grin got bigger. She pulled away and tossed the vibrator aside. She touched my skin again. The feeling was electric. My skin was so sensitive after those orgasms, but I couldn't get away. I didn't want to get away.

"Thank you." Even when Paige and I were having sex I'd never orgasmed like that. I don't think I even orgasmed like that in college.

She unclipped me from the cross and unbuckled the cuffs. I fell into her arms and spent the night curled up next to her on her bed.

The following morning over tea and scrambled eggs, I asked her what one had to do for the "one-week intensive" that Kathy had referred to.

"Depends. Is that what you want?"

"I don't know."

CHAPTER SIX

Stevie

I never knew what to expect from a newbie, which was always part of the thrill. One concern was a sort of buyer's remorse. Another was that some newbies might have these really high expectations of what would happen, and if the experience didn't meet their expectations, they would be disappointed to say the least. Megan was fabulous. There was something about her that convinced me that she would have no regrets, that there was a good chance she would be back, that she might be ready for something far rougher than what we did the other night. I hoped so. I was soft and easy about letting her orgasm. I wanted her to work harder for any future ones if we played again. Kathy was right. It might be time for a new wench to add to the family. Megan might be the one. Maybe.

But for the moment, I had to focus on Kathy and Britney, who had arrived to play this afternoon. I was sitting on the sofa while they were on their knees in front of me. They were naked and facing each other with their hands cuffed behind their backs. I had placed clips and chains on their nipples, belly buttons and snatches so that they were linked to each other. The chains hung slack between them, but every so often they went taut, and they moaned and groaned. Periodically I would yank on one of the chains. The one that ran from Kathy's clit to Britney's elicited quite a bit of teeth gritting and gasping. Neither one of them was allowed to come yet, and the first one to fall wouldn't get to come at all today. The winner in this little bout would be rewarded with multiple orgasms.

I sat back on the sofa and watched them struggle. Both of them were straining against the leather cuffs that bound their wrists while trying to maintain their balance. Kathy was trying in vain to blow away a stray hair that was tickling her cheek. They were both so well trained that they didn't even speak without permission unless they needed to use their safewords. Still, I liked checking in and hearing their voices.

"Kathy, tell me what you're feeling."

She told me that her quads were burning, and her nipples were throbbing. She bit her lip as I reached over and gave the chain linking her left nipple to Britney's right another quick yank.

"Britney, your turn." I leaned back and stuck my hand down my leather pants.

She told me how wet she was getting and how her clit was pulsating. Her shoulders were starting to ache because her arms were pulled back and her wrists were tightly cuffed.

"You're not coming, are you?" It was a rhetorical question, and we both knew it. She also knew she had to answer.

"No, Sir."

I reached my hand into my own wetness as they continued to gasp and struggle for balance, such a beautiful sight. A bead of sweat rolled down Kathy's forehead, and Britney started to pant. That usually meant she was trying to forestall an orgasm. She knew if she kept it at bay that there might be an even better one or more waiting for her.

Kathy's thighs started to shake, and then they gave out. She fell toward me, yanking the clips off of Britney's nipples. Britney let out a squeal.

I hadn't come yet, but I had an idea.

I pulled my hands out of my pants, which I took off so my lower half was naked. I kept on my leather vest and T-shirt. Kathy laid there on the floor, panting and writhing. Britney kept kneeling with a smug smile on her face and rightfully so. She wouldn't be disappointed she had forestalled her orgasm and, more importantly, maintained her balance.

I yanked on the chain and clamp left hanging from Kathy's nipple, pulling it off. She moaned again and kept trying to get back up.

"Stay there," I barked. Britney still had a clamp and chain hanging from one nipple and another hanging from her clit. She had a big smile on her face, but it was time for some humility. "And you, head down."

She obeyed.

I wish I could better describe the joy of dominating someone, especially two beautiful women. It just made me feel so strong and powerful. Bottom line: it really turned me on, and we had only just begun.

I unlocked Kathy's cuffs and told her to crawl to the playroom and back, bringing the metal chastity belt and bra with her. This gave Britney and me a moment alone. I went over to her, wrapped my fist around her long black hair, and yanked her head back. She grunted. My wenches made the most beautiful sounds. I quickly pulled off the chain hanging from her nipple and the one off her clit, triggering a couple more squeals.

"You get to come today, but you still don't get to until I say you can. Get it?" I pulled her head farther back, and she let loose a sound I barely recognized, a mix of a low grunt and a growl. We both knew what the answer was, but she tried to nod yes with the little movement her head was still able to do with her hair wrapped so tightly in my fist.

"What will make you come today, bitch?"

"You, Sir, just you, Sir."

I loved it when my wenches devised their own torture, even if they didn't know it. She would come today by my hand, as she requested, but only after Kathy had driven her crazy under my direction.

I lowered my lips to hers, and she opened up to me. She knew better than to ever close anything to me. When she was like this in my house, all of her was mine. My tongue dove into her mouth until she gagged. I ran my tongue along her teeth. My lips pressed hard against hers. I slapped her breast with my free hand. Her tit bounced against the stinging slap. Her black skin was warm to the touch. The slapping made it even hotter. She jerked. I grabbed her nipple and squeezed as tight as I could. She squealed and saliva ran down the side of her mouth. I pulled away when Kathy came back, dragging the chastity belt and bra. The metal chains clanged loudly against the floor.

I directed Kathy to stand. I wrapped the steel bra around her chest and padlocked it at the back. Pink padding protected her flesh from the metal's sharp edges. Attached rings would have allowed me to chain her up in various uncomfortable positions, but I decided to forego that today. I ordered her to step into the chastity belt. This device covered most of her snatch and all of her clit. I pushed the built-in clear rubber dildo into her cunt. It filled her hole. The device had a couple of gaps to allow her to take care of her bodily functions. Another padlock at the front secured it tight. I dropped the keys in a drawer in a side table.

"Remember where those keys are," I said. "You'll need them when you come back tomorrow to get unlocked. But for now, I need you to finish what I started. You interrupted me."

I grabbed the chain around her neck, pulled her back down to her knees and took a seat on the sofa. I pointed to my snatch, still wet with my juices.

She dove in, running her tongue up and down my cunt. She rubbed her nose in my pubic hair. She sucked on my clit and made it even harder. I dug my hands into her hair and pushed her farther into me. The cold metal of her chastity gear brushed against my legs, turning me on even more. I imagined her nipples getting harder against the metal bra, her clit pushing against the chastity belt. She would not be released until tomorrow, and she knew it. She ate my cunt hungrily and being unable to get release would keep her insatiable for the rest of the day.

She was exactly where I wanted her. Britney stared at us, still on her knees, still with her wrists bound, her shoulders pulled back. Her tits, a large pair of dew drops with dark areolas, stuck out. She squirmed. She knew how much I liked a good show. I knew how much she enjoyed watching one of my wenches serve me like this. She had a bit of the voyeur in her. I held my orgasm back for as long as I could because I wanted to test Britney's discipline. Would she be able to wait until I gave her permission to come? I heard her whimper. Kathy moaned, her mouth full of my cunt.

Finally, I orgasmed with great spasms running from my toes to my head as Kathy ran her tongue around the opening of my pussy. I pulled her head away and pushed her to the ground.

"You did a beautiful job, Kathy."

She smiled but stayed on the floor waiting for my next command.

I put my leather pants back on and grabbed my black leather biker boots from the corner of the living room. I liked the sound the heels made against my hardwood floors. When I returned to my lovely ladies they had barely moved. Feeling generous, I decided Britney could make a request. I grabbed her by the throat, applying just enough pressure, so she knew my hand was there.

"How do you want me to make you come, bitch? What will make you scream?"

She gasped. "Wax and ice, Sir."

I directed Kathy to get a bowl of ice cubes, a box of Shabbat candles and a lighter. I wasn't Jewish, but I had learned wax play from a nice Jewish girl. Shabbat candles were pure paraffin with no perfume. They dropped beautiful dollops of hot wax on her olive-toned skin. She even invited me to go to synagogue with her one Friday night. I liked the service, but I hadn't seen her in ages.

When Kathy arrived with the supplies, I had her set them up on the end table. Then I noticed that Britney was no longer kneeling. Her quads must have finally given out. Too bad, but I hadn't given her permission to get comfortable.

"On your knees, bitch!"

She quickly complied, but her thighs were shaking. I needed to back off a little to keep the scene going. I unhooked Britney's cuffs and directed her to lie on the floor. The smell of the sweet wetness emanating from her snatch hit my nose. She probably could have come right then and there without even touching her if I had just told her to orgasm, but I wanted to play some more.

I took a seat on the sofa and directed Kathy to light one of the candles. Candle in hand, she drew a line of dripped wax from the beginning of Britney's cleavage and down her belly, just stopping short of her snatch. Her pussy hair was closely cropped, and the hair formed a small rectangle around her slit. I nodded for Kathy to keep going. Britney kept writhing and groaning as the drops of hot wax landed on her snatch.

"Do you want to come, Britney?"

"Yes, Sir."

"Not yet. You said only I could make you come, so you will only come by my hand." Her face fell when she realized that she couldn't come by Kathy's touch, only mine.

"I don't know how much more I can take." Her eyes kept closing. Her body undulated, as though it was bouncing on waves. She didn't know where to move.

"We'll just have to see." I knew she could take so much more.

The candle burned down to almost a nub, and Britney was covered in wax. Kathy started pulling it off. I directed her to take her time when she started pulling off the wax on Britney's labial lips. The skin was delicate but pulling the wax off slowly meant that Kathy was painfully pulling out Britney's little hairs in her pubic landing strip. Britney was loving it.

"Please, Sir, let me come."

I ignored her plea. "Kathy, get the ice."

Kathy grabbed the bowl. The cubes had melted a little, but there was just enough for what I needed, for what Britney needed. Kathy rubbed the cubes over Britney's neck and down her shoulders. Britney moaned continuously. She wasn't screaming yet, but she would soon enough. Kathy took extra time and care rubbing the ice cubes around Britney's recently clipped nipples. They were tender and sensitive.

"Oh, please, Sir." Her pleas were getting louder.

I didn't bother to respond. I was enjoying the show so much. Kathy was locked into her chastity restraints. Britney knew she had to delay her orgasm even longer. I had both of them just where I wanted them. Kathy grabbed another ice cube and ran it down Britney's belly. She traced Britney's slit and then spread her labial lips. One finger grazed Britney's clit. Britney, the poor thing, let loose a little scream. Then the ice cube touched it.

"Oh God! Please, Sir." It looked like she was trying to get away from the ice, yet her face held an exquisite look of desire.

Kathy plunged an ice cube into Britney's hole and left it there.

"One more candle. Then it's my turn." I spread my legs and rested one of my hands on my thigh.

Britney looked relieved that her orgasm was not that far away, but

I still had big plans for her. Kathy once again traced the same path with the wax, but this time Britney's skin was cold. I knew it was that much more intense. She kept trying to get away while her gasps and pleadings for release got louder. This time when the wax started dripping on Britney's snatch, I instructed Kathy to stay in that spot. Britney's snatch became covered in layers of wax, and she started to scream. She started promising me that she would do anything I wanted if I would just let her come.

That was my cue. Standing up, I grabbed a vibrator and instructed Kathy to move away from Britney. I crouched near Britney and touched the vibrator to one nipple and then the other. "Are you ready to come?" I said in my deepest butch growl.

"Yes, Sir. Oh, please."

"Well, you better start screaming."

And she did. She begged. She pleaded for permission to come until she lost her words and only beautiful screams came out of her mouth. I moved the vibrator to her wax covered snatch. I pulled apart her lips. The wax cracked, and I touched the vibrator to her clit.

"You may come."

She bucked as one and then another and then another orgasm ran through her body. I directed Kathy to hold her as I kept the vibrator on Britney's clit until she begged me to stop.

When I was convinced that truly her last orgasm for the day had been had, I pulled the vibrator away. Britney laid there in Kathy's arms with a big smile on her face. She looked angelic, with her eyes closed. As her heavy panting turned into slow breathing, I sat down cross-legged beside her and started peeling off the last of the wax from her body. I knew how sensitive her snatch was so I didn't touch that. She would clean that later.

We sat there on the living room floor. I gave Kathy permission to get us some milk and cookies. I then held Britney in my arms as she slowly came down. Her skin was warm. She kept thanking me, and I thanked her. I was lucky to have her in my life.

We moved to the sofa and snuggled. Kathy joined us with the drinks and snacks. Her chastity restraints made things a little awkward but not impossible. I knew her nipples would have burst out of that metal bra if they could. Her juices were most likely making a puddle in her chastity belt.

"How do you guys feel?" I asked.

In response, Britney just cooed and snuggled her head more tightly against the leather vest that covered my breasts.

"I want to come," said Kathy, who snuggled on my other side.

"Maybe tomorrow if I'm in the mood when you come back to get unlocked." I took a bite of the butterscotch and chocolate cookies she had made. I gave her a big smile and a kiss on her forehead. She knew I wouldn't give in today even if she begged, although that would be wonderful for me to watch and would just make things worse for her. I had to stick by the rules I had stated. I may have been a kind top, but I wasn't soft.

We watched a few more episodes of *Orange Is the New Black* and this Australian web series I liked called *Starting From...Now*. I told them about playing with Megan. I told them how she secretly bound her hands when she masturbated and how I bound her to the St. Andrew's Cross in the playroom.

"We didn't do anything too hot and heavy, a little bondage, a little orgasm control, lots of talking. She seemed to like it," I said.

"Do you want to play with her again?" said Kathy, squirming on the sofa. She was desperate to touch herself or have me touch her, but that wasn't possible. There was no way for her to get relief, but she kept trying.

"She doesn't know what she wants. That's always dangerous. She could say she wants one thing, change her mind and then blame me. But, yeah, I think I do want to play with her again."

CHAPTER SEVEN

Megan

My breakfast that morning was more confusing than usual. I wasn't a big fan of dinner for breakfast, but I had cold pizza with a fried egg on the side.

"Are you sure Stevie didn't impregnate you?" Jane eyed my unusual-for-me breakfast as she ate her traditional toaster waffle and peanut butter.

I was eating what I craved and, yes, it reflected my confusion. I had no idea what my life held next for me. I assured Jane that there was zero chance of pregnancy. She mentioned that a Facebook friend of hers had posted a room for rent in her apartment that could be perfect for me. I had been camping out on Jane's sofa for two weeks, and she was dropping increasingly blatant hints about me finding a place of my own.

I didn't blame her. Jane and I were good friends, but all friendships had limits. I was getting close to ours. Jane's place was only a small one-bedroom. It really wasn't big enough for the both of us, and, more importantly, it was her home, not ours, not mine. I was grateful for her hospitality, but I promised I'd take a look at the posting if she sent it to me. I also felt the pressure of needing to find a new job. I'd sent out a lot of resumes, although no calls yet.

And then there was Paige. She still lurked on the fringes of the chaos that was now my life. Her latest strategy to try to get me to talk to her was to call or text and tell me which item of mine she was throwing out. Very passive aggressive. The pink sparkly high heels that I had worn on our first anniversary were in the trash. My collection of Agatha Christie novels had been donated to the local senior center.

"Don't you understand how much this hurts me?" she said on her voicemail. "It breaks my heart that you won't talk to me."

It's like she was the parent who, while spanking a naughty child says, "This hurts *me* more than it hurts you." Ugh. I really wasn't ready to talk to her. Truth be told, there was something freeing about the fact that nearly everything I owned fit into one suitcase. I could live without the sparkly shoes, cute as they were. I'd read the Agatha Christies a couple of times now. If I wanted to have them again, I could buy them. I could go to the library. Maybe there was stuff in our—make that her—place that I would eventually want, but trying to get it right now just had too high a price attached.

Jane left for work, and the day stretched out before me. I cleaned up from breakfast and ran the vacuum in the living room. Jane was such a great host. I wanted to be a good guest.

My mother called. I informed her that, no, I did not yet have a job. She encouraged me, in that needling way she sometimes has, to be nicer.

"Nicer to whom, Mom? Paige? Potential employers? Myself?" I didn't give her the chance to come up with an answer. "I gotta run and go be nice to someone."

While I checked my email inbox for replies to my job search, I thought about Stevie. I felt so calm with her. I liked being with her. I just wasn't sure if what she had to offer was what I really wanted. I wasn't convinced that the kind of stuff she did was really me or just some deranged fantasy that should stay unfulfilled. It had been a week since we'd had sex. I hadn't called her, and she hadn't called me.

On my midday errands run, I bought some fresh bread and salad for our dinner, but some construction on the way home meant I ended up on a street different from my usual route. It was on that street that I spotted a sex toy shop. The windows were not blacked out. Actually, the window display had a lot of pink in it. I decided to go in. I'd never been to one of these places. The toys I'd bought to spice up my non-existent sex life with Paige had been purchased online and arrived in plain brown wrappers.

The shop was small. A butch woman with red curly hair was behind the counter. I told her I was just looking and prayed she wouldn't ask me too many questions. I touched the restraints, the chains, and the paddles. I ran my finger along the leather and felt the cold of the metal. The clerk seemed to hit a perfect balance between being watchful and leaving me be. I was the one who broke the silence.

I held up a thick black leather collar. "What if I don't like it?"

"We do take returns on some items if they are returned in unworn condition." She grinned. She seemed like a patient person, like I wasn't the first newbie she'd encountered in the shop.

"But what if I change my mind about being tied up?"

"A good top will untie you and not tie you up again."

"But what if I really like it?"

"You still get to decide if that's something you want to do again."

I continued looking around and bought a paperback copy of *The Story of O* and a tiny vibrator. The book I remembered as being despised by my women's studies professor at university. The vibrator had a cute pink and black argyle pattern on it. I didn't need it and couldn't afford it, but I felt like I should buy something. The woman threw a lube sample into the bag and said to come back any time.

"I'm always happy to answer questions."

As she passed me my bag, our hands touched for just a moment. I wondered if she touched everyone like that or just me, but I knew I needed more of that. I needed someone to touch me like Stevie had done last week.

When I got home, I started making dinner—a couple of pork chops with sautéed kale and potatoes on the side. As the meat sizzled, I dialed Stevie's number.

"Hi, it's Megan."

"Megan. Hello."

That voice of hers. I trembled a little. I pushed the kale around the frying pan far more than it needed to calm myself down. I flipped the pork chops a few times. *Remember to breathe, Megan*, I told myself.

"So, what's up Megan? Do you need something?"

"I'd like to see you again." A lump filled my throat. I felt Stevie's cuffs around my wrists and ankles again even though they were long gone.

"Okay, you can come on over."

"I'd like to stay for a week."

"A week? Oh, yes. Kathy told me that she mentioned my little one-week intensive to you. Do you know what that involves?"

More silence. A deep breath. A mild tingle in my snatch.

"Well, you all seem so happy. I want that. I want what you have. I want to submit to you for a week and see if this is for me. I want to know if it is me. I don't know if it is."

"When do you want to come over?"

She sounded pleased but cautious, and I didn't blame her. I didn't really know what I wanted. I didn't even have a job at the moment. I didn't have a home, but it was time for me to take a risk, possibly the biggest risk I'd ever taken. I hoped learning whether I liked what Stevie did or not would reset my life in some way.

I told Stevie that I would come by after dinner and after I had talked to Jane. She said she would be ready for me. Tonight would involve a lot of talking, she said. She asked me what I wanted.

"Something completely different."

"I can do that."

In between cooking, I packed up my things. I was far more orderly than when I threw stuff in my suitcase while trying to get out of Paige's home. By the time Jane got home, my bag was by the door and dinner was on the table.

"You called my Facebook friend. Wow! That was fast!"

"No, I'm going to spend a week with Stevie."

She furrowed her brow as she put away her work stuff and switched to comfortable shoes. "You know you don't have to rush out of here."

"I know, but this is something I want to do."

I had so many mixed feelings as we ate dinner. I was sorry to be leaving Jane. We really had been having fun over the past couple of weeks, despite all the chaos. I was terrified about spending more time with Stevie. I was ready to move on with my life. I just wasn't sure this was the direction I necessarily wanted it to go.

Jane kept assuring me that I could change my mind at any time. Yes, she did want me to move out and move on, but she was my friend. She wanted me to be safe. I promised we would have some contact at least once a day.

"You better! And these pork chops are delicious."

I put all my stuff in the trunk of my car and set off for Stevie's. I thought about how our lives move forward and move back, but not really. You can't ever really go back to anything. Change is constant.

When I arrived at Stevie's, we sat on the sofa. She talked about the week she liked to spend with her wenches. Yes, there would be a lot of sex and hearing that made me happy. But it was more about getting to know each other.

"You may even get to know yourself better," she said.

There were women she played with occasionally, but she regarded her wenches, the women she played with regularly, as family. She asked me loads of questions about what I liked and what I wanted and what I was attracted to and what turned me off. She talked about hard and soft limits and safewords. She talked about saying red, yellow or green to indicate what I was feeling and whether she should stop, slow down or keep going.

I didn't know the answers to most of the questions, but she promised that by the end of the week I would be able to answer them all. I told her I wanted to submit to her.

She smiled a little. "This week is about discovery. We may discover that we're not meant to be with each other. We may discover that we belong with each other. You never know until you try. One thing I can promise you is that by the end of the week, you'll truly know what submitting means."

"Are we supposed to have some kind of contract?"

"We can put something in writing if that makes you more comfortable." She placed her hand on my knee and gave it a squeeze. "I've always just preferred talking things out as we go along. Trust that I will always respect your safeword, and I will always respect you, even when you are at your most vulnerable."

She made me feel so safe. I felt that way with Paige, at least at first. I knew on the second date that I wanted to be with her for the rest of my life, but it was the safety of familiarity. She had long hair like me and pale skin. We looked like a beautiful all-American couple.

She promised me a white picket fence. She talked about marriage. Every weekday we worked 9-5. We left and arrived home at the same time, although we went to different office buildings. Every Friday night we ate dinner at a restaurant, frequently the same one we had eaten at the week before. On Saturday night we ate in, and, until the past year, we would have sex. We didn't involve toys until I got them in a vain attempt to restart our sex life, and there was a dishonesty that ran deep through our relationship that I didn't recognize until recently.

"Ever thought about settling down with just one woman?" I asked.

"Nah. Not for me."

I loved her honesty, but I wondered if I could change that as she told me to get naked and put all of my things in one of her closets.

"You won't need most of that stuff this week."

I told her about my deal with Jane and the vibrator I had bought that afternoon. She had me take out the vibrator and give it to her. She promised to use it on me at some point. She said I could get my phone as needed.

"This is not a hostage situation. That closet is not locked. You can leave at any time. You have willingly agreed to stay with me for a week. Never forget that. You have a lot of power and responsibility in this situation. You don't get to just lie back and think of England."

I wondered about her statements as she put cuffs on my wrists and ankles and a temporary collar around my neck. The buckle was at the back, but I could undo it myself. The smell of leather was strong. I thought about what it meant to submit to her but still have responsibility for myself. I thought about what it meant to make decisions and judgments about the sex I was having while submitting to her.

"Permanent collars are locked and only I can remove them." She gave my collar a little tug.

For the first time in a couple of weeks, my life felt like it had some stability. I liked the feeling of black leather against my neck. I liked my nakedness in her presence. That night, once again, I slept in her strong arms.

In the morning, my eyes opened before hers did. I got out of bed and cleaned myself up to get ready for the day, although there wasn't that much to do since I was naked and I didn't expect to wear clothes that day. I stared at myself in the bathroom mirror. I was still me. My hair was still long and soft. I still had a small dimple to the right of my mouth. My eyes were still brown. My smile looked the same, but I was naked in a bathroom that was not mine. The collar had left a small red mark under my chin, most likely where I had pressed on it during the night. The metal rings on my wrist cuffs banged against the vanity. I was still me, but it was a version I'd never seen before.

When I returned to the bedroom, Stevie was awake.

"Hey, beautiful." She smiled drowsily. "What's for breakfast?"

I hemmed and hawed. We hadn't really discussed breakfast.

Her smile faded slightly. "Submitting to me means more than just doing what I say. It means submitting to my needs. I won't punish you because it's your first day. I really do hate punishment. But you need to get downstairs and make me some breakfast. When I get downstairs, I expect it to be ready and for you to be on your knees waiting for me." She flipped over in bed and turned her back to me.

Yes, indeed, this was a new version of me. I wanted to be with Stevie. I wanted to submit to her. I wanted and needed to know how.

Once in the kitchen, I realized there were a few things I didn't know and not knowing heightened the tension I felt. I didn't know how much time I had before she would come downstairs. I didn't even know what she wanted for breakfast. I scrounged around in the kitchen. *Not much here*, I thought. *Someone needs to do the grocery shopping. Maybe that'll be me?* I found two bagels, cream cheese and smoked salmon. I started the kettle for tea. I poured us both glasses of orange juice. When the second bagel popped out of the toaster, I heard her coming downstairs. I put together two plates. Each one had a bagel and the trimmings. I took a seat.

I looked at her with an expectant smile and tried to present the breakfast like I was Vanna White. She didn't look happy, more puzzled actually, and then I remembered. I was supposed to be on my knees. I started to get up.

"Don't move." She sounded stern. Hers was a voice I wouldn't dare disobey, at least not voluntarily.

I stayed still as she clipped each of my wrists to an arm of the chair and each of my ankles to a chair leg. So that's what those metal loops were for on this chair. They were not merely decoration. I couldn't move. I couldn't close my legs, but I started to speak.

"Shhh." She put her hand over my mouth.

I had to admit I was scared, but the restraints felt so good. Her hand felt so soft.

"What color are you now, Megan?"

My snatch was wet. She removed her hand from my mouth. "I'm green," I said softly as she took a seat in front of her breakfast. I was hungry. I hadn't eaten since last night's dinner, but she explained that she always ate first unless she said otherwise.

"There are privileges to being on top." She picked up one half of the toasted bagel from her plate. "You got this toasted the way I like it. There are privileges to submitting, too. I hope you discover them." She bit into the bagel half.

"I'm hungry. I want to come." My movements were limited, but I started to squirm as best I could.

She swallowed and took a swig of orange juice. "Good to know. You've made a good breakfast. You'll eat soon, although if you talk too much I'll gag you. I don't know if you'll come today."

I sat there smelling my toasted bagel. It was getting colder as it sat on a plate right in front of me. There was no way for me to undo the clips on the chair myself and be able to reach the food. I got the impression that Stevie wanted some quiet, and I didn't want to be gagged, at least not yet. I was hungry. Gags intrigued me, though. I wanted to try one. In between bites, she reached over and pinched one of my nipples or dipped her fingers in my snatch.

She flicked my clit with her thumb. "Remember. You can't come until I give you permission. And I might not give it today. Maybe not the whole week."

I moaned with desire and in frustration.

When she finished her breakfast, she unclipped my wrists from the chair and clipped them to each other. "You like being bound, don't you?" She ran her fingers through my hair.

I nodded yes as I ate. It was the best bagel I'd had in years. The dough was a little chewier than usual. The salmon was just a little bit saltier. The cream cheese seemed richer than ever. None of that was true, but I was hungry and bound and everything tasted better.

CHAPTER EIGHT

Stevie

Megan had been too demanding this morning, but I knew I could change that. She would learn. I have a stable of well-trained wenches, and I was beginning to think that Megan would make a nice addition. I just had to treat her right. I really started falling for her when I learned she was ticklish. It was our first afternoon together. I dressed in my leathers, and I again clipped her to the St. Andrew's Cross. This time I set it up so she could not escape by her own hand, and I told her so.

"If you need to get free, you have to ask for it," I said. "What color are you?"

"I'm green." She tugged on the restraints and smiled.

There wasn't a mark on her body yet, and she was green in more ways than one. When I do a first week with a wench, I consistently escalate the amount of trust we have to have for each other and the amount of responsibility we have for ourselves. The sensations become more intense. The situations have higher stakes and can be challenging even for someone with a lot of BDSM experience. Megan didn't have that experience. Before meeting me, she had only tied her hands to masturbate. She'd never played with anyone else, but she was so hungry for it.

I enjoyed watching her, the way her biceps flexed when she pulled against her bound wrists, the way her calves moved when she pulled against her similarly bound ankles. Her hair was thicker than Kathy's. Her breasts were a little perkier than Britney's. They bounced as she struggled. The scent emanating from her snatch told me she was turned on and very wet.

Megan had a belly button that stuck out a little like Jodi, the Jewish woman who taught me about Shabbat candles. She was the first woman I'd spent a full week with quite a few years ago. After years of dabbling in BDSM and leather sex, I was ready to dive into it full on and embrace the fact that I was a butch top and a damn good one at that. I'd tried vanilla sex, and it did not get me wet. I'd tried being more feminine.

One night, after several hours at the salon, I went to a local gay bar for a drink. A drag queen looked at me and said, "Honey, a butch in a dress is still a butch in a dress. That weave fits you like bad drag." I spent that evening ripping out the extensions I had spent so much time and money on. I threw out the one dress I had.

When I met Jodi a few days later at a friend's party, my head was shaved. She told me how handsome I looked, and I went home with her. She kept asking me to bite down harder on her nipples. I did and spanked her ass with my bare hand. I got very wet.

I asked her to submit to me for a full week. She did so with glee and abandon, and I became the butch top I was always meant to be. I bought my first leather vest that week and changed my name from Stephanie to Stevie.

We broke up in part because she wanted monogamy. I didn't have that to offer. I tried it once, but monogamy just never suited me. I felt more like a hostage than a girlfriend. I have a lot of love to give. I have a lot of love I want to receive. It's not that I'm always looking for something better or different. I just always want more. I see no reason to be miserly with myself or any other woman I'm attracted to.

Jodi was willing to accept that for a while, but then she wanted to top me. I didn't want to switch. I still don't. I can dish out a lot more than I can take. For that reason, I have so much respect for my wenches. Their capacity for pain amazes me every single time we play. Not allowing her to top me was the final straw that ended that relationship, although I think of her fondly. I wonder how she's doing, and I'm always grateful for what she taught me.

Like the fact that one solid week together can change your world.

I hoped it would change Megan into an amazing wench because right now she was very close to getting gagged. She was being a pushy bottom. Too much talking.

"I'm ready to take whatever you've got. Bring it on." She chattered along those lines and pulled on the restraints. She clearly didn't know much about BDSM, but she was putting on a good show.

"Looks like I'll need to gag you."

"Bring it on. I can take it." She was downright defiant. I don't know where she learned that or where she got the idea that it was the right thing to do. That was going to have to change.

I grabbed the gag from the shelf, the one with the large red ball for Megan to sink her teeth into. She opened her mouth without hesitation. Bring it on indeed. I wrapped the device around her head.

I stood back and crossed my arms across my chest. "Say your safeword. Tell me how you feel now."

She couldn't. I expected that, but I wanted to make sure she knew what the gag took away from her, although she could still have some limited communication. She didn't look scared, but she certainly didn't look like she was going to try to tell me what to do, at least for the moment.

"Bark like a dog," I said.

She did as ordered and a line of drool started to drip from the right side of her mouth.

"When you're gagged, that's your safeword."

She tossed her head back and forth and started to moan. Her bondage held her tight. I stepped closer to her, keeping my eyes locked on hers. I plunged my fingers into her snatch. She was good and slippery. I plunged one finger and then another into her hole. She squealed louder. I pulled away and brought my fingers to my nose and then hers. She smelled sweet and was getting sweeter.

"Do you want to come today?"

She nodded.

Of course she did. I sat down in my leather chair. I reminded her that I got to come first. She only got to come if I gave her permission. I unzipped my leather pants and stuck my hand into my own wetness. Watching Megan struggle was really turning me on. It's understandable to be hesitant about newbies, but there's also something so attractive about them. Everything amazes them.

I told her about my first paddle, which was hidden behind the toy rack. I didn't use it very often anymore. I'd made it myself senior year of high school in woodshop and used it to paddle my first girlfriend. We were both 18 and so young. She ended up not finding it appealing, but I did. I held onto it and pulled it out whenever a vanilla girlfriend was willing to give it a try. I had many other paddles to choose from now, but for the longest time it was my only one. It still gave quite a whack, but I was so sentimental about it that I was afraid to use it. I didn't want it to break. Megan listened attentively, as if she could do anything else. I came in great gasps, and then let loose a sigh.

I approached Megan again. I ran my hand down her tautly bound arms, and when I was running my fingers along her armpit, she let loose a muffled giggle from behind her gag. I realized something. She was ticklish. I couldn't remember the last time I'd been with someone who was ticklish. This was going to be fun.

I ran my fingers down from the cuff on her right wrist and down her arm. I lingered and fluttered my fingers wherever she started to giggle and squeal. The inside of her elbow, her armpit and the right side of her belly were all prime spots that made her buck and struggle and make all sorts of interesting noises. The left side produced similar results. I ran my fingers all over her body like I was playing the piano. She even let loose a few screams. Delicious.

"You want me inside you? You want to come?"

She nodded again. She breathed heavily behind her gag. Her body was a pure white canvas for me to paint. I couldn't help admiring it.

"Does this room still scare you, Megan?"

This time she shook her head, no. I was sure she would have said more if she could. She was a talker. I thought I saw a hint of a smile. There was probably a more complicated answer in her.

"Excellent." I let the word fall out of my mouth stretching out the syllables.

My playroom smelled of rich leather, dark wood and Megan's sweat. I ran my fingers across her belly, prompting her to buck and giggle again. I jammed one finger into her snatch and pulled it out quickly. I was deliberately rough. Her moan told me that she liked it. I plunged two fingers in, again fast and rough. Another moan.

There's a myth about tops that we always know what we're going to do. We always seem so calm and suave as some lovely gives us control. The truth is sometimes we're as unsure as anyone else. I kept running my hands over Megan's bare skin. She was so green, so unmarked, and she was giving herself to me. She wanted to submit but didn't know how. I felt so honored. I had just a glimmer of what she liked, and so did she. We were both learning so much.

I grabbed her vibrator from the shelf. So cute and pink. It suited her. I turned it on, feeling the vibrations run up my arm. I touched her cheek with it and moved down to her ticklish armpit, triggering a loud squeal. I touched it to her erect nipples before pinching each one tightly. If she could have smiled, I think she would have. Her moans got louder. I ran the vibrator across her ticklish belly. She was so beautiful writhing on my cross. I circled her belly button. Again, I plunged two fingers into her snatch, but this time I had the vibrator in my hand. I held it on her clit. She started breathing more quickly. I removed my hand.

"It's time for some pain first," I whispered in her ear. To send home my point, I bit her earlobe. Her eyes closed. Her teeth dug a little deeper into the ball gag. She made some indescribable noises, but she seemed ecstatic.

Ah, but how to dispense the pain I wanted to give, the pain Megan seemed so hungry for. I grabbed some nipple clamps. I tightened one on her left nipple until Megan's squeals went up an octave. If her squeals went any higher, only a dog would be able to hear them. I ran the chain through a loop in her collar and then placed the remaining clamp on her right nipple. The chain was taut, and her breasts were elevated. She tried to relieve some of the tension by lowering her head and neck, but it didn't do much good. Every time she wriggled a clamp got pulled harder. She was causing her own pain. I could probably cause more.

I watched her eyes widen as I walked over to my whips, floggers and paddles. She started to whimper. I wondered if she was holding back an orgasm. I hoped she was. Her breasts were almost floating. She might have been wincing, but I wasn't sure.

I grabbed a dark brown paddle with holes drilled into it. That one always gave such a satisfying whack. I moved the cold wood against her skin, just barely grazing her creamy flesh. I thought about how it would leave bright red marks on her belly, but, no, not today. It was just our first day. I wanted to save something for later in the week, but I wanted her to know what was coming. Next, I touched her skin with a paddle with a crosshatch pattern and sharp points like a meat tenderizer. That was the one that left beautiful bruises my wenches treasured for days. No, it was too early for me to mark her body. I put that one away, too. I wouldn't use any of those toys on Megan today.

No, it was her nipples that called to me. I unclamped one and then the other, and the clamps dangled from the chain running through the ring on her collar. I wasn't done with her nipples yet. Her breathing became fast and rough. I put my mouth on her left nipple and bit down hard. She screamed, although it was somewhat muffled by the gag. I grabbed her right nipple between my fingers and squeezed. She started to buck against the cross. I reapplied the nipple clamps.

It was time for her to come and to really scream.

I stood in front of her with my legs in a wide stance. I turned on the little vibrator.

"Are you ready?" I used my deepest, scariest voice.

She whimpered some more. Her eyes pleaded. She nodded, a move that I knew caused her breasts pain because of the clamps. She was so hungry and so ready.

I wanted to hear how much. I stepped closer to her and brought the vibrator near her face. I whipped off the gag, glistening with saliva.

"Thank you," she managed to gasp.

I grabbed her hair, pulling her head back and making her yelp as the clamps pulled harder on her breasts.

"It's time for you to call me, Sir, if you still want to come." I saw rivulets of sweat running down her neck. "Do you want to come?"

The words came out slowly, but they came.

"Yes, Sir. Please, Sir." Her voice was a notch above a whisper.

I let go of her head to give her some relief and lowered my hand, the one with the buzzing vibrator, to her snatch. I was close enough for her to feel it, but not close enough for her to come. She was so wet.

"Please, Sir. I really want to come."

Some of the defiance from earlier was gone. I plunged my hand into her snatch, and she screamed. "Do it now, bitch. Do it before I get tired or bored."

It was moments like this that reminded me how much I loved being a top. She probably would have done anything for an orgasm.

She let loose another yell, as I held the vibrator on her clit and pushed three fingers into her. She was wet and wide open. It was breathtaking seeing her buck and thrash against the cross as she came. She really had been holding a lot in for very long time, long before she met me. Her vagina tightened around my fingers.

"Oh, please, Sir. Please, stop. I can't…"

"No. One more scream, bitch."

She let loose with all her might. I removed my hand from her dripping cunt. She hung on the cross gasping as I threw the vibrator in the dirty toy bin. I slowly removed the nipple clamps, each one triggering a beautiful grimace as blood flowed back into the nipple. Next, I unclipped her from the cross. She fell at my feet in a shuddering heap, still gasping from the experience.

"Thank you, Sir," she said with her arms wrapped around my shins. Her face was wet as she kissed my feet. "That was amazing." She stayed down there for just a moment breathing heavily. I helped her up. Her skin was warm and sensitive. I held her hand and led her to the bathroom where I wiped her face.

I pointed to her image in the mirror. "Look how beautiful you are."

She was in a fragile, post scene state, and I wanted to take care of her. There was more to taking care of a sub after a scene than just rubbing salve where her cuffs and collar had rubbed. Now was the time to be gentle with both her body and mind. She blinked at the mirror like she didn't know what she was looking at. I stroked her hair and brushed my hand against her cheek, still hot from what she had just experienced. She moved her jaw like she couldn't find words.

"So beautiful," I repeated. She seemed to take my words in like a sponge.

We moved over to the sofa where she sat next to me eating

cookies as we watched an old episode of *The L Word*. She was nuzzling into my bosom when my doorbell rang.

It had to be Kathy.

I wrapped Megan tighter in her blanket and got the door.

Kathy sashayed in, wearing a loose blouse and a skirt, a little different from her usual wardrobe. It wasn't easy to find something that looked good over metal chastity restraints. I got comfortable on the sofa again and signaled Kathy to strip. She did with obvious pleasure, revealing the steel bra and the chastity belt. She shifted from foot to foot. She was so antsy. She probably would have come if I just breathed lightly on the right spot.

"She lost a bet," I told Megan who cooed softly in reply. She disappeared a little more into what was increasingly becoming a blanket nest. I turned back to Kathy. "How much do you want to come, bitch?"

At that she dropped to her knees and kissed my feet. She wrapped her arms around my legs and begged. She said she loved me and would do anything for me. She whimpered at my feet.

Wow. Two women whimpering at my feet in one day. Life was so good.

"Time to get the keys." I was looking forward to this as much as Kathy was.

Kathy opened the drawer on the nearby side table and presented to me the keys to her freedom like they were objects of great veneration such as religious relics. She kept her head and, more importantly, her eyes down. She was all mine.

"You're such a good bitch." I grabbed the keys from her hands and turned to Megan. "Maybe someday, you'll be this submissive." I'm not sure Megan heard me, but she looked so peaceful and happy.

I turned back to Kathy who was fidgeting and waiting. She was always so patient, but I knew it was a struggle. I told her to stand, and she rose. I loved looking at her when she was like this, at her most perfect, at her most desperate.

I walked behind her and undid the lock at the back of her bra. I imagined how hard it must have been for her to sleep last night, starving for orgasm with hard metal against her skin. She gasped as I removed the bra, and her breasts fell out. Her nipples were hard and bright pink. I stayed behind her and reached around to the lock holding the chastity belt at the front. I pulled on it a few times so the metal would dig into her skin. She let loose an unusually high squeal.

"Please, Sir." Her voice was breathy and timid.

She knew I honored only a limited number of requests. I didn't have much patience for pushy bottoms, like Megan had been earlier. Kathy didn't say more. I undid the lock. The belt slid down to the ground, pulling out the dildo that had been in her snatch for the past day. A wicked smell hit my nose, mix of salt, sweat and desire. One of my hands reached around to pinch a nipple. It was so tender she yelped. I pushed my other hand into her snatch.

"If you are ready to come, bitch, do it or I'll lock you up again." I moved my fingers back and forth over her clit and played with her hole.

She screamed something unintelligible and started to shake. It was like the orgasm, having been trapped for a day, didn't know what to do now that it could be free.

I tightened my grip on her nipple, and she screamed again. I kept diddling her snatch.

"Please!" she said.

"You know you can come. Let it go. Let it flow."

Whatever was holding that orgasm back crumbled.

She gasped and sobbed as the orgasm ran through her like a brushfire on a hot summer night. I pulled away my hand, and she kept spasming until she collapsed in my arms. I pulled her over to the sofa, and she curled up next to Megan. They dozed off next to each other while I went to the kitchen to make myself another cup of tea.

After Kathy had gone home, Megan had a quick phone call with her friend Jane. I guessed that she probably had promised that she'd check in with her friend every day or something. Later, we talked about what she liked about the day and what she didn't. She was such a blank slate and so new to this. I wanted her preferences to become stronger, more defined. I wanted her to know herself. I wanted to know her.

CHAPTER NINE

Megan

I didn't know what I was going to make for breakfast on my second morning with Stevie. I just knew I had to make it. I could hear Stevie getting ready upstairs. I didn't have much time.

After getting the coffee started, I found some waffles in the freezer that I popped into the toaster. I could still feel Stevie's fingers inside me. My nipples were sore. I was still reeling from yesterday. I'd never had an orgasm like that before, and I wanted more. I loved being bound. I loved the nipple clamps. I wasn't sure about the tickling, but I did want to be spanked. I wanted to see how much I could take.

I wasn't sure about the gag either, but it definitely sent me into an unfamiliar head space. I was acutely aware of every moment. Last night after dinner Stevie explained the concept of "pushy bottom." I could understand why it was so unappealing to her. I wasn't sure it appealed to me either. I wanted to submit, and it didn't sound like submission. I didn't even know why I did so much talking yesterday. I suspect I was nervous.

I heard Stevie's footsteps on the stairs. She was wearing her heavy boots, and the sound reverberated through the walls. I got on my knees by her chair. The toaster waffles popped. The coffee pot finished brewing, filling the air with a dark aroma, but I stayed there waiting. I kept my eyes down and my arms behind my back. All I saw was the floor, and her shadow coming near. She grabbed me by the hair until I was standing.

"Good job. Get up and finish breakfast." Her voice was gentle, but firm. The black leather vest she was wearing with nothing underneath barely hid her breasts.

She kissed me and then sat down and started scrolling through the news on her phone. The city council was considering regulating short term apartment rentals. A man was shot on the other side of town. A new artisanal coffee shop was going to open down the street.

I hadn't been outside in more than 36 hours. I wasn't sure I cared what was going on in the outside world.

I served her black coffee, orange juice and two waffles. After that, I stood beside her and waited. My stomach rumbled, but I knew I needed patience. When she finished, she handed me her plate to put in the sink and signaled me to sit down to eat my own breakfast. As I ate, she asked for my thoughts on yesterday. She was amused by my reaction to being gagged but seemed pleased that I liked being bound so much.

"You should be bound more often." She got up from the table. "Let's take care of that."

She opened a drawer and grabbed a wide leather belt. She wrapped it around my middle and the chair and locked it at the back. I could still move my arms. I could finish my breakfast, but the belt was so tight that I could barely breathe. The food went down slowly. The leather was thick and heavy. My snatch got moist.

Still standing behind me, she wrapped her hand around my neck, constricting my breathing even more.

"In this house for this week, I can control everything about you," she whispered in my ear before taking her seat again. My wetness made me squirm a little. I ate carefully and slowly as she read more headlines about war and strife around the world. Occasionally, she showed me a cute animal video that popped up in her feed.

"Tell me what color you are now," she ordered.

"Green. I'm definitely green."

I settled into my seat which did nothing to loosen the belt's grip on my midsection. It reminded me of the belts I used to cinch around myself in my college dorm room, but it was so much wider. It was clearly designed to restrict and nothing else. And it wasn't buckled at the back. It was locked with a heavy padlock. She placed the key in a saucer at the other end of the table out of my reach.

"Can we talk?" I asked in between labored breaths. I loved what was happening, but I needed some questions answered.

"Sure."

"Without getting gagged?" I put my knife and fork down and took a swig of orange juice.

She nodded.

As turned on as I was, I felt like I should tell her about my doubts, about my shame. I hated admitting I liked what I did, what she did.

"Paige, my ex, used to call me sex-obsessed."

"You're not sex-obsessed just because you like sex." She put down her phone and put her hand on top of mine. She didn't grab or squeeze. Her hand just lay there, radiating warmth.

"For a year we didn't have sex. She barely touched me." A tear rolled down my cheek. I'd tried so hard not to think of Paige, but I felt more than naked with Stevie. My recently broken heart was right at the surface. Stevie stood up, kissed me and wiped my cheek.

"It's okay," Stevie said. "It's all okay."

"I loved nearly everything you did to me yesterday. I love what you're doing to me now. But why do you like this? Why do I like this?"

"I was just born this way, I guess. I can't answer that question for you. You have to do that yourself. Do you want me to remove the binding belt?"

"No. I want to be under your control. I can't believe I said that out loud. I wish I knew why. I wish I didn't feel so ashamed." I squirmed a little, mainly to confirm, again, that my movements were very restricted in this belt. The more I squirmed, the more turned on I became.

She kissed me again. This time deeply. My mouth was open. I wanted to be completely open to her.

When she pulled away, she patted my head and told me to finish my breakfast. "Eat up. You'll need it. Sex, even rough sex, especially rough sex, can bring up feelings and emotions. This week can be overwhelming."

I asked her how many girls had lasted a whole week with her. She said about a dozen. I asked her how many started a week with her and didn't finish.

"No one."

"Is there anyone else coming here today?" I asked as I finished my food.

She shook her head. "Just the two of us today. How does that sound?"

I realized that there was one other thing from yesterday that I wasn't sure about. I wasn't sure about being with Stevie and other women at the same time, although it seemed like yesterday was a special occasion. I wasn't sure about the non-monogamy that seemed to be such a good fit for Stevie, but that's what this week was for. I got to figure out what I really liked, whether it was nipple clamps or being part of someone's gaggle of girls rather than their one and only.

"Have you ever thought about being monogamous?" I asked.

"No."

And that ended that discussion.

I sat there for a moment, the empty plate in front of me, the black leather strap digging into my belly. "Sir, I'd like to be spanked today."

She smiled and grabbed the keys that would unlock me. I smiled back. I did have my doubts, but I wanted to test them. I wanted to test me.

She released the belt. I took in great gulps of air.

"We will play today, just the two of us. That will be your reward for a job well done."

She directed me to tidy up the kitchen and then told me that my job every day for the rest of the week was to clean whatever toys were in the barrel in the playroom. I was to take care of this every morning. I did so, scrubbing some vibrators in the hottest water possible and boiling a pot of dildos on the stove. She then directed me to air dry the toys on a towel spread out on the sideboard. As they dried, she inspected each one. I had to re-wash a red corkscrew dildo, but everything else passed on the first try.

"Good job. Ready for more?"

"Yes." I hoped she didn't mean more cleaning. She didn't. She directed me to get on all fours. The tiles were cold on my knees. When she pinched my still-sore nipples I yelped.

"They still hurt." I might have sounded a little whiny.

She yanked harder on my tender nipples. "Until I tell you otherwise from this point on you will only speak when spoken to or I'll gag you again. Do you understand?"

I nodded. She pinched my nipples even tighter. The waves of painful pleasure ran down my body.

"I asked you a direct question. You need to answer it properly. You are to speak when spoken to."

"Yes." The sensations triggered when she pinched my nipples made me sway a little. I had to concentrate hard to keep from falling over. She yanked my nipples again.

"Properly," she barked.

Properly. Oh. "Yes, Sir."

She let go of my nipples.

I didn't know it was possible, but today was more intense than the day before. She attached a leash to my collar and led me to the playroom.

Honestly, I felt shame at my nakedness and being led around like a dog, but I felt safe with Stevie. I was exactly where I was supposed to be. I was trusting her to lead me in more ways than one.

"How badly do you want to be spanked?"

I looked up at her standing over me. Her nipples were big and firm, peeking out from her leather vest. A pair of black leather jeans and the heavy boots that made so much noise completed the look. Just a few weeks before, before I broke up with Paige, before I lost my job, before everything changed, I would have looked at Stevie with derision. She was too butch. "What kind of lesbian wants a woman who looks like a man?" I would have said. "What kind of freak is into all that leather and kinky stuff?" I would have probably said that too.

But she was all the woman I wanted right now. The truth was I was that kind of lesbian, that kind of freak.

"I want it. I want my ass to burn. I want you to cause me pain."

"Why?"

"I don't know. I just do, Sir." I wondered what I had to do to truly get things started. The door to the playroom wasn't even open yet, and I was already wet. I had asked her unanswerable questions, and she was doing the same to me.

"When this is all over, you'll want more than that."

I didn't know what she meant, but she said it like I was about to learn a fabulous secret that was just for me. She opened the playroom door and directed me to the sawhorse. I didn't feel graceful as I clambered on. I wondered if there was a more sophisticated way to get on as if I'd done it a dozen times, but she kept telling me how beautiful I was. My breasts hung down over the middle beam. There were rings on the sawhorse that she could have clipped my cuffs to, but she didn't.

She took thick leather straps and wrapped one around the middle of each of my forearms. The buckle was far away from my fingers. There was no way I could get free until she let me go or I used my safeword. She applied similar straps to the middle of my calves. When she ran her fingers along the bottom of my feet, I bucked and squealed.

She laughed and told me again how beautiful I was. She grabbed my hair and pulled my head back. A vibrator was in her hand. She kissed me roughly as she pleasured herself.

"It's going to be a long time before you come," she growled after she came quickly and loudly.

I wanted to come, but at that moment I wanted to be hers, to exist for her, to be nothing but hers. I didn't want to be a pushy bottom. I was happy to know she would let me come eventually, and I was willing to wait.

She kept kissing me until her tongue made me gag, and her teeth on my lower lip made me squeal.

"What do you want?" She came again.

"You. I want you."

She just smiled, let go of my hair and took a seat in the giant chair reserved just for her.

"When will you learn?" She pleasured herself until she came again and again. "Maybe I won't let you come after all, but I'll still spank you because it's what I want."

And then I realized my mistake.

"Sir, please, I want you. Only you, Sir."

She laughed again and threw the vibrator in the dirty toy barrel. "I'll let you know if you can come." She grabbed a paddle off the wall. It was red on one side with black fur on the other.

The first slap was loud but felt soft. I got wetter still. In between slaps she would reach inside my cunt and pinch my clit. She ran the fur paddle along my labial lips, and I started to moan.

"That was my gentle paddle. I know you can take more." She returned the red paddle to its place and grabbed a small paddle made of medium brown wood with rows of holes drilled into it.

The first blow was softer than I expected, but then it turned out she was just warming me up. She alternated the paddle with her hand. It got to the point where barely knew which was which. Each blow stung. My ass was getting so hot.

She told me what a good bottom I was. That was not something I had ever aspired to, but I felt proud.

Next, she showed me her flogger, bringing it close to my face. She draped it slowly across my back. I could feel the softness of its leather. Then it landed with a furious and rapid sting on my already sore ass. The orgasm I'd been holding back threatened to erupt.

"No. Sir. No." I panted through gritted teeth.

She stepped back. "No is not a safeword. At least it's not ours. What's going on, bitch? Answer me."

"Sir, I can't stop the orgasm. I don't know what to do. Should I call yellow? I don't want you to stop or slow down."

Her hot breath was electric on my ear. She whispered, "I know what to do. Hold on. I know you can do it." She stroked my hair. She ran a gentle finger down my back.

She grabbed a black velvet bag hanging from a hook on the wall and poured the contents into a little pile on the side table. Clothespins. I didn't have to wonder for long how they would help me forestall the orgasm that I didn't have permission to have and that I desperately wanted to hold back.

First, she applied one pin to my engorged clit with a sharp snap. Then another. The orgasm was still there, but now it was caged. Trapped and straining. Then she used the clothespins to clip shut my labial lips.

She grabbed my hair and pulled my head back. "Is that better, bitch?"

"Yes, Sir." I realized that I wasn't being entirely honest, but I wanted to be. Stevie wanted me honest. "I don't know, Sir."

She gave me some water and told me I would know when I

needed to.

"But first I'm not done with your ass, bitch." She slapped my raw flesh with her bare hand and then went to the little fridge. "Do you know what I like?" She took out an ice tray.

"No, Sir."

"To hear a woman scream. To hear a woman beg. To have a woman give me everything she's got. Let's see what more you've got."

She rubbed an ice cube on my poor red ass until the cold was painful. I wasn't quite ready to scream, so I wasn't quite sure what to do. I knew better than to ask. I hadn't been spoken to. She stuck an ice-cold finger in my ass. That made me moan.

She grabbed the flogger again. The first swing made me scream as the tails hit my increasingly raw flesh. The cold made my already reddened skin so sensitive, but it did not break. I screamed even louder every time the flogger hit my ass.

"Beg for it, bitch. Let me hear what you've got left."

I don't know how many times the flogger struck me, but each time was excruciating. Sweat made my hair stick to my face. I was screaming so much that my throat started to hurt. My lips were dripping with saliva. She wasn't touching my nipples, but they started to throb with memories of the day before. My clit was ready to explode, but it couldn't. A dull ache filled my groin. Every so often she would take a break from the flogger and run her fingers from my armpit down my side, and I would laugh and scream. Periodically, I would find my words again.

"Please, Sir, let me come. Let me go. I don't know how much more I can take."

"I make that decision." The flogger landed on my ass again and again.

"Please, Sir," I yelled and pulled on the leather restraints until they dug into my flesh. "I'll do anything, Sir. Anything."

The flogger stopped, and she kissed my ass gently. Her soft hand stroked my back, making me shiver. She pulled hard on one of the clothespins gripping my labial lips until it let go. Then she pulled off another and another until my dripping cunt was open and waiting for her.

Her voice took a softer, kinder tone. "You can come any time after my hand touches your clit."

But she didn't go there first. She went for my vaginal opening. I didn't scream. I didn't think I had any screaming left. I just kept whispering.

"Please, Sir. Let me come. Please," I said as she stuck one finger in my hole and then another until she had three moving back and forth. Then I felt her thumb on my clit.

The orgasm was instant and magical as she rubbed back and forth and side to side. Its power ran through me like a tropical storm. I strained against the leather straps. I tried to get away from her hand, but I could not. And still she kept rubbing. The storm turned into a fire and then a sledgehammer against my insides. Everything was in a knot.

At last, she removed her hand. She was not touching me. She was probably standing right behind me, but I didn't care. Honestly, I wasn't aware of much of anything. All I knew was that my clit was still vibrating, my ass burning. I couldn't seem to get out of my mouth the stray hair that seemed stuck on my tongue. The leather straps on my calves and forearms felt comforting, like I was being held. The cuffs on my wrists and ankles were a reminder of who I wanted to be: Stevie's wench.

A cold glass of water came to my lips, and I drank, awkwardly because of how I was bound, but I drank. The water was fresh and clean, tinged only slightly by the salty sweat on my lips. I gulped it down. I'd never been so thirsty. Water had never tasted so good. She put her hand on my back as I drank. It felt light as a leaf.

When she took the glass away, I breathed in deeply. I smelled leather and sweat and my own juices. I smelled Stevie, a mix of barely scented body lotion and her own sweat.

I don't know how long I lay there being held by the sawhorse and the leather straps, but my stomach started to growl.

"Are you ready for me to let you go?" she asked.

"Yes, Sir." I was regaining my voice, but I still could only speak in a whisper. The shame I was feeling around liking the sex that I did—and it was becoming increasingly clear that I really liked it—was fading. It was replaced by a joy unlike anything I had ever felt.

Stevie released the straps one by one and helped me off the sawhorse. I was wobbly and unsteady. She held onto me, brushing my hair out of my eyes. She wiped my face with a soft towel. She applied salve to my ass and my nipples and anywhere the leather straps had cut in. After we moved to the sofa, I curled up half asleep in a blanket, and she covered my body with soft kisses.

I had Stevie to myself for the rest of the day. I knew she wasn't interested in monogamy. I had to admit that I was, and I was so happy it was just the two of us.

That night I curled up in her arms and cried. I cried for Paige and the other women I had loved and lost, but most of all I cried for me. I released the sadness that had been buried deeply in secret corners of my heart and let it all go.

CHAPTER TEN

Stevie

As I lay in bed listening to Megan getting breakfast ready, I knew today would have to be gentle. This was her third day in my house. I needed a break as much as she did. My bicep and tricep on my right arm were sore from paddling her ass the day before. She was able to take more than I expected, and I was just plain tired. I'd been having a lot of good sex lately, but even I needed a day off.

I got up and opened my closet doors. I stroked one of my leather vests, inhaling its rich scent. As tired as I was, I loved the reminder of yesterday's session with Megan, but I would not be wearing that today. I threw on a T-shirt and shorts. When I came down, Megan was on her knees waiting for me. She looked so beautiful and calm, a different woman from the screamer who jumped on Bud Red a few weeks ago. She was quiet. Her eyes were down. Her chestnut brown hair cascaded down her bare shoulders. The red on her ass from yesterday had faded but was still visible.

This morning she had made scrambled eggs with cherry tomatoes and onions. I think I also tasted a little pepper. Pretty good. I'd never been much of a cook, so a welcome byproduct of having my wenches was that I often ate well. As she took my plate, I offered her a cushion so she could sit down and enjoy her breakfast. She thanked me with an extraordinary smile. I loved seeing her smile. Yes, today would be a quieter day.

She told me how she liked it when I pulled her hair, and her love for bondage and spanking was limitless. She liked the kissing. She liked just about everything from yesterday except being led around on a leash while she was on her knees. That was certainly negotiable. We didn't have to do it if she wasn't into it.

"Sir, my ass feels...my ass feels still warm." She scooped up a forkful of eggs and put it into her mouth. "I can still feel where you bound me, but my nipples have recovered from a couple of days ago. I can't believe I'm saying this out loud, but I like how I feel." She spread her arms wide like a kid seeing her first Christmas tree.

"You know, you don't have to call me Sir unless we're in a scene. You can call me Stevie. It's up to you."

She nodded and went back to eating.

We had a lovely lazy Monday morning. Megan squirmed on her sore ass. The cushion only provided limited relief. She finished breakfast and cleaned up from both our meal and yesterday's play. When she sat back down, I clipped her cuffs to the metal loops on the chair, so she was bound and happy. I read her some news from the outside world.

A bomb had exploded in a busy Middle Eastern market, killing dozens. Federal officials were taking action on sexual assault on university campuses. NASA posted some cool photos of Jupiter. A new leather women's party was starting at a local bar. An exhibit of photographs of butch women in the 1920s would be opening at a downtown gallery.

When Kathy showed up after lunch with a package—wow, we really were having a lazy day—I thought I saw Megan's smile fade, ever so briefly, but then I was distracted by what Kathy had brought over. When I turned back to Megan, she didn't look any different. She smiled at me like she had all morning. I wondered if I was being too sensitive.

Kathy opened the box and unfurled a mass of dark pink latex.

I'd always been a leather gal, but Kathy was recently getting into rubber. I wasn't sure about rubber, although I was having fun exploring it with her. The smell was both smooth and sharp, and I loved the range of colors, which you really didn't get as much with leather. Maybe it wasn't my thing, but I could see the appeal.

"It's a gimp suit. I want to try it." Kathy ran her hand against the rubber, as if smoothing it out.

"We're in the middle of our week," I said, motioning to Megan. "And we're taking an easy day."

"Oh, come on. It's just arrived." Kathy cajoled and begged.

She really had me wrapped around her little finger. Of all my wenches, she was probably the best at pushing my buttons. She knew how much to push and when.

I really wanted to, even though I was tired, and it was Megan's week. I wanted to take care of Megan.

Then Megan spoke after trying so hard to look docile with her still pink ass resting on a cushion that Kathy was very familiar with and pulling against her restraints just to remind herself that they were still there.

"I'd like to try it," Megan said. "This week is about me figuring out what I like, and us getting to know each other. I'd like to try it."

There was something so delicate about her voice.

Kathy looked surprised for a moment and then pleased. "I love that idea!" she exclaimed.

Kathy and I hadn't topped anyone together in quite a while. So much for a quiet day.

I told Megan to start calling me Sir again, and that we would play in the living room. Kathy squealed and dashed to the playroom to pick out some toys.

Megan hadn't liked crawling on her knees on a leash, so I unhooked her from the chair and told her to walk upright to the living room. There she would wait for us on her knees. I dashed upstairs to change into my leathers. By the time I got back, Kathy had changed to a strapless purple rubber dress that was in stark contrast to her white skin and showed off her cleavage. Several toys were spread out on the side table. Megan was on her knees waiting.

I figured we could do just about anything except hit her ass. That area definitely needed a break. The morning quiet period seemed to be enough for both of us. We were ready to go.

Kathy showed us the gimp suit. The attached hood only had holes for Megan to breathe through her nose. She wouldn't be able to see or talk. The hood would fit snugly around her head, hiding her beauty and even muffling her hearing a little.

"This is real sensory deprivation." I pulled her head up so that she could see what she was about to get into. "And you're going to have to really trust me. Are you ready? You're going to have to give me even more total control over you than before."

"Yes, Sir." She sounded convinced, and so was I. When a bottom truly trusts a top with her life and a top trusts a bottom, there's nothing sweeter.

The rest of the suit would encase Megan's body. Her arms would be squeezed into short sleeves that would force them to bend at the elbows. Her hands would grab her shoulders. Her legs would be similarly bent at the knees. She would be able to move, but awkwardly on her elbows and knees. There were pads in the suit to protect those joints, but she wouldn't be getting very far very fast.

I directed Kathy to take off Megan's collar and her wrist and ankle cuffs. I didn't want them to snag or tear the latex. Kathy rubbed Megan's skin where the leather restraints had dug into her flesh. Megan looked bemused, like Kathy was removing something that had always been there rather than something that had just been put on a few days ago.

My eyes roamed over Megan's naked body before I gave her nipples a quick pinch. She winced.

"How are your nipples?"

"They're ready for you, Sir. I'm green."

"Oh, good!" Kathy really was excited about playing with me and Megan in rubber.

I promised Megan that we would be extra careful with her ass, but all else was fair game. She agreed. I also told her she could come as much as she wanted. She seemed happy about that, but some lessons can only be learned the hard way. She was about to learn how intense one unstoppable orgasm after another could feel. An orgasm could make a person scream as much as a flogger on a bare red ass.

Kathy helped Megan into the suit, which had a long zipper along the belly. Once Megan was in, she clomped clumsily around the living room. I prevented her from bumping into furniture while Kathy grabbed a baby blue vibrator that she had picked out from the playroom. I stroked Megan's head feeling the pattern of her hair encased in the rubber hood.

GIVE ME THORNS

I thought about breath play. I could have briefly blocked and unblocked her nostrils and then changed my mind. We'd already done some of that the day before. Megan had liked it, but today was supposed to be easy. I didn't want things to get too intense, especially when she couldn't give a safeword. Plus, this rubber gimp suit was new for both of us.

I ran my hand down her back, which seemed to calm her. She stopped fidgeting. She stayed at my feet like a dark pink Jeff Koons sculpture. She really did remind me of his giant metal sculptures of balloon animals come to life. I could hear the low rush of air going in and out of her nostrils, but she was otherwise silent and so beautiful.

She flinched when Kathy applied the vibrator to her neck. I held Megan fast and told her what a good bottom she was and how pretty she looked in latex.

Truly she did. The latex gripped the glorious curves of her breasts and her ass.

Kathy ran the vibrator, really one of my lower-powered toys, gently over Megan's back. She stuck it in one of Megan's armpits and ran it down her side, eliciting a muffled giggle, or at least I think it was a giggle.

"Did I mention she was ticklish?" I said to Kathy.

Her smile got bigger, and her eyes lit up as she ran the vibrator down Megan's other side. Megan bucked and squealed. I wondered what was going through her head. I would find that out later, but for now she had become our gimp. Faceless. Speechless. She couldn't see. She could only feel. I'd had women under my absolute control before, but this was more intense than anything I'd ever done.

It scared me a little. This was a great responsibility, but mostly I loved it. I straddled Megan between my legs, gripping her as tight as I could. I told her she was safe, although I didn't know how much she heard. The little blue vibrator in Kathy's hand made Megan spasm and yelp. I unzipped my pants and stuck my hand inside.

I was slick and slippery, turned on by my growing love for Megan and the gift of control over her life, body and pleasure that she was giving me. Kathy threw the vibrator aside, and I pulled her to me. Megan wriggled between my legs. I kissed Kathy deeply as I held her. She had such a beautiful twinkle in her eyes. The purple latex hugged her skin, hiding nothing. I was starting to appreciate the appeal of latex more and more with two women clad in the slick material.

Kathy grabbed the blue vibrator again and passed a small yellow one to me that I strapped onto my fingers. I had one arm around Kathy's waist and could feel her soft flesh beneath the cool rubber. My other hand was running the vibrator over Megan's body. The gimp suit had turned her into a giant pink blank slate. Her features were buried in the latex, but I knew she was there. Her breathing got heavier. Kathy and I turned Megan onto her back. Her limbs were short stubs, and her head lolled side to side. I placed the vibrator on one of her nipples and then the other. Her moans got louder. They got louder still when Kathy placed her vibrator on Megan's snatch.

Then Kathy got a devilish look in her eye and turned to the toys on the side table. I wondered what she was up to, but I didn't have to wonder long.

When she turned back to us, the low-powered blue vibrator was gone. I grinned when I saw that she had strapped my "old faithful" to the back of her hand. This vibrator was a monster, and I knew what it could do. An oldie from the 1950s that I'd bought years ago at an estate sale, it consisted of a large metal motor that strapped to one's hand through a set of springs. It plugged in, which limited its reach a little, but the cord was long enough to allow the vibrator to get the job done and then some. A metal toggle switch at the back turned it on. If you looked closely at the motor, you could see sparks fly. I put down the vibrator I had been using on Megan. That little thing was totally unnecessary now.

I crouched down and braced Megan's shoulders between my legs. I stroked the slick latex that hugged her skin and told her what a beautiful bottom she was even though I couldn't see her face or her smile. I told her I was falling in love with her.

"Cowabunga!" yelled Kathy as she knelt and placed the vibrator on Megan's body.

Megan bucked and thrashed, but she couldn't get away. She was trapped by latex. She was safe in my embrace.

Kathy put the vibrator to Megan's nipples. Megan's squeals got louder. The thrashing became stronger.

Kathy knew well the power that this vibrator had. I had used it on her many times. She could feel it now in her hand and running up her arm.

"Now let's see how often she'll come." She ran the vibrator down Megan's belly to her snatch. She kept it there. Megan's squeals turned into screams. She thrashed and bucked like a wild horse.

Kathy held the vibrator firm against Megan's pussy. Megan could not shake it off. Kathy then stuck her hand up her dress. As Megan came over and over again, so did Kathy with a giant grin. She called out to God with each climax.

"Can I get an amen?" I laughed.

"I love you, Stevie," Kathy said as Megan's sounds got louder.

"I love you, too."

Kathy removed the vibrator, but Megan was still writhing, trying to get away from the stimulation that was no longer there. It was the aftereffects of the vibrator, phantom vibrations. Slowly, her breathing returned to normal, and her moans and squeals stopped. When she was finally still, Kathy unzipped the gimp suit. Megan was covered in sweat and other fluids. She stayed curled up on the floor like a newborn.

By the time I kissed Kathy goodbye and sent her on her way, Megan had recovered a little, but she looked beyond exhausted. There was still something that seemed slightly off, but I chalked it up to post sex exhaustion and sub drop.

I asked her how much she heard in the suit as we lay in bed. She said she heard lots.

"I love you, too," she said as she drifted off to sleep.

CHAPTER ELEVEN

Megan

I woke up feeling unsettled on day four of my week with Stevie.

I looked at my wrists wrapped in the leather cuffs that were increasingly feeling like they were part of me. I could still feel the echo of the paddling that Stevie had given my ass a couple of days ago. I could smell pink latex from the day before. My clit had only just stopped vibrating from yesterday's multiple orgasms. Every day with Stevie had been more wonderful than the day before. She was giving me what no other woman ever had.

I looked over at Stevie. I listened to her slow breath easing in and out of her lungs. I stared at the closely shorn black hair that covered her head. I looked at how the blanket draped over her chest barely showing the outline of her lovely breasts. She had one leg outside the comforter. I marveled at the curves in her thigh and calf.

My phone call with Jane the night before had been my usual check-in. I reassured her every night that I was fine. Stevie was not a serial killer. She didn't hold women against their will. Jane told me about her latest jog, and how she was thinking about running a marathon. She told me about the gal at work who had just gotten a new job and was moving on, and how the company had cut curly fries from the cafeteria in a budget-cutting move.

She also told me something last night that hit my heart dead center. She had received an invitation to Paige and Lulu's wedding.

That was when I told her I had to go.

That conversation weighed heavy on me all night. I could still feel it this morning. We'd been broken up for barely three weeks, and she was getting married. I had wanted that for us. I wanted that for me. But first I needed to get up and make breakfast.

I toasted Stevie and me a couple of bagels and put them out on the kitchen table along with cream cheese and some fruit. I started the coffee pot. Then I got on my knees and waited. My ass was still tender, although it could probably take whacks again. Enough time had passed, but that tenderness reminded me of that day when I had Stevie to myself, of not sharing her with anyone else. I wanted her to myself again.

She came downstairs. She smiled and praised me for being a good bottom as she patted my head. I smiled but kept my head down.

She finished her breakfast and signaled me to eat mine.

I'd asked her more than once about monogamy. I'm not sure why I thought asking her again in a different way would elicit a different answer. I was probably hoping something had changed. Her answer made it clear that I had changed even though she hadn't.

We talked about what I liked and didn't like about the day before. I liked the gimp suit and the vibrator, but I preferred playing with just her. She nodded. I told her about my ex's impending nuptials and how much I'd like to get married someday. She said that she hoped I would find the right woman to do just that.

She leaned back in the chair, sipping her coffee. She pulled her tablet closer to her and began tapping and swiping on it until she settled on something to read. I watched her slender fingers as they moved dexterously across the surface of the tablet. I watched her as she read. I was really starting to appreciate her kind of beauty. A hard truth also hit me. Stevie was falling in love with me. I was falling in love with her, but this week I was getting in touch with what I really wanted. I expected to learn even more, but at that moment I knew she couldn't give me what I wanted, what I deserved.

"Excuse me. Stevie?"

She looked up and smiled faintly.

"I'm sorry, but I have to ask. Are there women who have sex like you who are monogamous? Who won't cheat?"

She assured me there were. She never cheated, but she couldn't do monogamy either. "Cheating means you're lying. I never lie."

"Am I not good enough?" I was holding onto the last shred of hope that I could do or say something to change her.

She looked genuinely puzzled. Then she got up and kissed me, holding my head in her hands. "You are good enough to have whatever you want. I'm just sorry I can't give you everything."

She sat back down. Except for the faint tick of the wall clock, the kitchen was so quiet. I ate slowly. The world felt still.

"I need to be outside today," I said after I took my last bite of the bagel. "I need some air."

Stevie's smile faded as I got up and went to the closet where she had stored my stuff.

"I want to come back, but I need to get out. I need to think."

She gave me a set of house keys and told me to come back any time. I got dressed but left most of my stuff with her. I wasn't quite ready to leave completely yet. I just knew I needed to go.

"Am I your first wench who hasn't made it through the week?" I asked as I stood at the front door.

"A full week of play is hard for anyone. Most take at least a small break in the middle. I'm impressed you lasted as long as you did. Besides, you'll be back. The week isn't over yet," she said as I walked away from her.

I sat in my car staring at the house where I'd spent the past four days. She stood at the open door looking at me. Occasionally, she broke into a soft smile. I knew I'd be back. I had to claim the rest of my stuff, and I didn't really have anywhere else to go. I loved sex with Stevie, but I wanted something she couldn't give me.

I drove around aimlessly for a while and then pulled into the parking lot at the library to call Jane. She was thrilled that I wanted to have lunch with her. She even apologized for wanting me to move out. I told her that was unnecessary. She was right. I needed to move on. I said I would tell her more when we got together.

We met up at a downtown Thai restaurant on her lunch break. She hugged me super tight.

"Need to breathe." I wheezed for dramatic effect.

She released me. "Sorry. I'm just so happy to see you."

I assured her I was fine as we took our seats. "I need to work some stuff out is all."

"Clearly. You left that house of horrors. Why are you still wearing these?" She pointed at my wrist cuffs and collar. My ankle cuffs were hidden by my jeans.

They felt so comfortable I hadn't even realized I was still wearing them. They had become more a part of me than I had realized, although they did explain some of the weird looks I had been getting since I re-entered the outside world.

I touched the cuff on my left wrist. "I'm not ready to take them off yet."

"I can't believe you're so into this stuff. And so into Stevie. I mean, she's nice enough, but…I don't get it," she said as our food arrived.

"Neither do I. I just know how she makes me feel." I took my first bite and looked around the restaurant. Most of the people were office workers dining alone or with one or two other people. A lesbian couple sat not too far away from us. They looked to be in the early stages of their relationship and only had eyes for each other.

I signaled to Jane that there were some Sapphic sisters nearby, and we gave them a we-know-you-are-and-we-are-too nod. Then they returned to staring into each other's eyes over an order of crab rangoon.

"I'm so confused," I said.

"That makes two of us." Jane did her best sneer and eye roll. "A butch woman and rough sex. Who are you? Seriously."

"I love sex with Stevie. I always felt safe with her. I trust her, but…"

"There's more to life than sex."

"You're right, but it's really important to me. Paige was the ice queen for the last year of our relationship. Now she's getting married? Ugh. I can't be happy for her. I loved her. It's not fair. I'm falling in love with Stevie. The sex is great, but she'll never really be mine." The metal loop on my cuff clanged against the table, and I took a deep breath. The guy in a suit at the next table gave me some side eye.

"We all have to make compromises. You'll never get everything you want," Jane said, serenely.

I loved Jane to death, but I hated when she got like this, so all-knowing and seemingly wise. What made it worse was that she was usually right.

"Couldn't I at least get the bare minimum?"

"Yeah, but first you need to figure out what your minimum is, and maybe not move quite so fast. You've had sex with Stevie. You think you love her. I think you did something similar with Paige. And every girl before her."

Ugh. Of course, she was right. I hated that. I responded by taking another bite of my chicken curry while she kept talking.

"And maybe by jumping so fast you're blocking something really great with someone who's just good enough."

I sighed and changed the subject. We talked about the women's professional basketball team that was being established in town and how much fun it would be to see a game. She talked about the dog she was still thinking of getting. She wanted one who would run with her.

As we finished our food she reached across the table and grabbed my hand.

"It's going to be okay, you know." She squeezed my hand. "Maybe you just need some time. And you can sleep at my place tonight if you want. Even if you're wearing these." She flicked her finger at the leather cuff still wrapped around my wrist.

I told her I'd let her know. We paid our bill, and she went back to work. I took a seat on a bench near the restaurant. The unusually cool spring had finally broken, ushering in pleasantly warm temperatures. The midday sun was bright, the cloudless sky a deep blue. After several days indoors and naked, I loved the feeling of the cotton of my T-shirt against my skin. A breeze gently grazed what little skin I did have exposed.

I got a few weird looks, but mostly I watched people walking by. There was a woman walking by in pink scrubs who looked like she was on her way to start her work shift. A Lance Armstrong wannabe pedaled past in red and black spandex. Three squirrels chased each other's tails around a nearby tree. A fire truck drove past with sirens blaring.

The world was noisy, but I felt so quiet. I guessed that made sense. I didn't have anywhere that I needed to be, although at some point I would have to decide where I would sleep tonight.

I'm not sure who saw whom first, but I broke into a large grin when a butch woman with curly red hair started walking toward me. It was the woman from the sex shop. She walked like a woman on a mission, and she was heading right for me. I scooted over and made room for her next to me on the bench.

She pointed to my collar. "Looks like you've had some of your questions answered. Figured a few things out."

"A few things, but not everything." I liked how it felt to have her sitting next to me. Her body heat radiated through her jeans and mine. Although I didn't even know her name, she felt like a friend.

"You'll never have everything figured out. Life is such an adventure."

"But I didn't want it to be." And then the floodgates opened. I confessed the nasty things my friends and I had said about butch women, about leather women, about women who slept around, about women who didn't have good jobs, about women who didn't want a white picket fence, marriage and 2.1 kids, about anyone who took what we thought were "stupid" risks.

"I haven't taken a lot of risks in my life, but I am now and it scares me. I think what I want doesn't match what I think I should want, what is respectable."

She didn't interrupt me, so I just kept going. "I fell in love with Paige. She was professional and femme and vanilla. We were totally respectable. I wanted to marry her. Now she's marrying the woman who she was having an affair with when she was with me. I've fallen in love with a woman who gave me these cuffs and collar. She's butch. The sex is amazing. She'll love me, but she'll never marry me. She'll never be mine and only mine."

I had to stop and take a deep breath. She put her hand on my thigh. My fingers found hers. The touch that I remembered from a few days ago at her shop lingered. She held my hand lightly. I didn't feel grabbed. I felt held.

She told me her name was Simone. She was named after her grandfather, but her mother wanted something fancier and more feminine than Simon. This close I could see the way her nose was angled ever so slightly to the left and turned up at the end. I wondered what her lips would feel like if I kissed her.

"If you're looking for feminine respectability, I'm the wrong person. I mean, I work in a sex shop. I had a respectable job once. It really wasn't for me."

"I'm increasingly realizing that respectability is overrated."

Her face inched closer to me. Her lips touched mine ever so gently. It was barely a kiss. I knew it didn't make any sense, but I felt like I was cheating on Stevie. I pulled back.

"What's wrong? Too soon? I'm sorry. I should have asked if that would be okay."

I laughed a little. "That would have been the respectable thing to do, wouldn't it?"

She laughed louder than I had, a hearty, joyful laugh. "I suppose it would have been."

"You know, I just need someone to talk to right now. Is that okay?"

She nodded and kept holding my hand. It looked like she was really listening as I rambled on about losing friends every time I got into a relationship, about always moving too fast, about loving leather and rubber sex. I liked being a good bottom, but I wanted monogamy. I wanted marriage.

She smiled, nodded at all the right times and patted my hand. "I need to go open the shop. Want to come with me? No funny stuff. Promise. Just come hang out while I set up."

"Would you tell me about everything?"

She said she would.

When we got to the shop, we did something that I hadn't done in a long time. That afternoon we were just two friends having fun. She explained the meanings of the various flags. The black and blue flag with a red heart turned out to be a leather pride flag. I had no idea there even was such a thing as leather pride. I doubted that if I'd known what it meant when I saw it on the back of Stevie's helmet that I would have gone with her that night. But maybe I would have? I was so ready for life to change. There was a rubber pride flag, too, with yellow, red and black diagonal stripes.

"Can you be both?" I asked.

She assured me I could be both and moved on to explaining the bear pride flag with stripes in shades of brown and a claw. I recognized it from Stevie's fridge.

"Why would a lesbian have that flag?"

"She might have bear friends. Maybe she identifies as a bear in some way? You'll have to ask her."

She showed me various paddles, restraints and gags. She told me about tying her hands together when she masturbated in her college dorm room.

"Oh my God, I did that, too!" I exclaimed.

"Yep, I knew what I needed," she said.

She told me about the first time she ever paddled someone. She had just graduated from college and moved to a new town. She met someone online, and they went to her place. The woman paddled Simone first.

"That was okay, but I really loved it when she put the paddle in my hand and turned her butt to me. She kept getting louder and louder and her ass got redder and redder. It was so beautiful."

I played with the multiple buckles on a leather sleep sack. I tried on a leather jacket and modeled it for Simone. She said it suited me. She told me about the Ace of Clubs, a monthly lesbian leather party at a local dungeon that was this Friday night.

"You're welcome to come. We love it when new women show up."

It sounded intriguing, but I wasn't sure. "I want to talk to Stevie first."

I went through the nipple pasties and thought that I would like to wear a pair for Simone. I bet she'd appreciate them, too, in a way that Paige or any of my previous girlfriends couldn't. I was amazed at the incredible range of dildos and vibrators. The super huge ones scared me and not in a good way. She recommended a long purple dildo that felt cushy to the touch.

I handed it back to her. "You know what I'm really afraid of? I'm afraid that if I'm with Stevie, it'll block me from what's really right for me."

Simone was dusting one of the displays. "That's always a possibility."

I grabbed one of the paddles, a large dark wood one with little heart-shaped holes.

"Is there anyone who will tie me up and hit me with something like this, but only with me? Someone who will be mine?"

She grabbed the paddle out of my hands and spanked her palm a few times with it. It made a very satisfying thwack sound. "Yeah. Me."

We stood there staring at each other. I still had on Stevie's cuffs and collar. I wasn't quite ready to take them off, but that moment was getting closer. I could feel it.

The first customer of the day came in, which I took as my cue to leave. I was going home to Stevie, and I knew exactly what I needed to do.

CHAPTER TWELVE

Stevie

I stood at my front door watching Megan drive away as the postman parked on the block and got ready to deliver our mail. The flowers across the street were starting to bloom, and it looked like one of the neighbors had bought a new car. Or maybe they had a guest on this sunny Wednesday morning who had driven here in a purple Mustang convertible with wire rims. As one of the few people on our street who was home on weekdays, I had become the *de facto* neighborhood watch. Everything looked as it should, but I was already missing Megan.

We'd been having such a good time, such good sex. Sure, she could be too talky, but she was learning and a gag solved that problem fairly quickly. What was amazing about her, though, was that she could take pain like someone who had bottomed for years.

I closed the door behind me and got on with my day. I checked my investments to make sure they were earning the money I enjoyed and needed—they were and then some—and started planning my next vacation. I was dithering about traveling to Europe. I hadn't been to Paris in such a long time, but I was in the mood to see the Mona Lisa and walk along the Seine one more time. Also, my little French wench, Mireille, was getting impatient to see me again. I smiled at the memory of her. Or I could take Bud Red on a road trip and see where I ended up. Hadn't done that in a while either, and I was overdue.

At lunch I looked at the empty chair beside me. No clang of Megan's restraints accompanied the roasted turkey sandwich I ate. I knew spending a whole week with me was intense. Everyone who ever started a week with me finished it, but Megan was not the first one to take a break in the middle. She wouldn't be the last. I needed a break sometimes, too.

I hoped she came back soon.

There are so many myths about tops like me. People think we're always smooth and confident. We never get sad. We never get our hearts broken. We know what a bottom wants and needs without even asking. The truth was that I was sad that Megan wasn't here. I really wanted her to become a full member of my family. Given her desire for monogamy, I doubted that was going to happen.

I didn't need to be all that sharp to realize that I couldn't give Megan what she wanted. I didn't even think I could give that to Michelle Obama if she asked me for it, and she was one of the most powerful and beautiful women in the world. I loved her biceps. Megan was pretty special, too. A week with me is always about learning if someone is a fit for me and if I'm a fit for them. Megan and I were so sexually compatible, and believe me, sexual compatibility could be elusive. She was so beautiful. I loved the way her long silky hair fell over her eyes and how, when she was sweaty and bound in some way, strands would form sticky swirls on her pale skin.

If I promised Megan marriage and monogamy what about Kathy, April, Britney and my other women? How could I give myself to just one? It wouldn't be fair to any of us, least of all Megan. She needed someone, deserved someone who could love her honestly, the way she wanted to be loved.

I decided to distract myself with some fiction. I was in the middle of my old beat-up paperback copy of *Frankenstein* when I heard a key turn in the lock. My heart jumped a little. I was filled with joy when it turned out to be Megan. She was still wearing my cuffs and collar. Her cheeks were slightly red from being outside. She looked like she'd gotten some sun. She came and sat next to me on the sofa. We had a little small talk before she got serious. She spoke quickly like she had to get the words out before they escaped from her.

"My life fell apart a few weeks ago," she said as I brushed a stray hair from her face. "I didn't know what I wanted. I just knew something had to change. You came along out of nowhere. You swept me off my feet and showed me things I'd barely imagined. You were right that a week like this means learning what you really want, learning who you are. I want to be with you. I want this kind of sex, but I don't want to share you. There. I said it."

She looked me directly in the eye. We sat in silence, letting her words soak into our pores. When someone like Megan who has no idea what she truly wants figures out her desires, it's glorious.

"I can't give you what you want," I said.

She nodded and started taking off one of the wrist cuffs. I put my hand on top of hers. I didn't want things to end just yet, and they didn't have to.

"Finish the week. Just a few more days. We can play and hang out tomorrow. I want to go to a lesbian dungeon night, the Ace of Clubs, on Friday night. I want you to come with me."

Megan paused and then slipped the leather strap back into the buckle. The black leather was stark against her white skin. Her forearm was covered with a layer of fine hair. Two freckles dotted her arm.

"I don't think I'll stay after the week ends. Are you sure you don't want me to just leave now?" She bit her bottom lip and lowered her eyes like someone who thought she was in trouble, like someone who was scared.

"I'm absolutely sure. I've fallen in love with you, but maybe we were meant to be friends rather than lovers, maybe we were just meant to play, but not get too serious. You don't even have to sleep with me tonight. You could sleep in one of the guest rooms. There's a lot of space in this house. And you don't have to get naked if you don't want to."

She looked at me with those deep brown eyes. She seemed newly awake and refreshed. "Will you bind me tomorrow? I'll sleep in the guest room, but I want to come with you again. I'd like that. I'd like it if we were friends."

So would I, and I told her so. But I knew what was going on. I wanted her total submission like I got from Kathy, April and Britney, but she was holding back for something that was clearly important to her, even if she didn't know who would give it to her. I have so much respect for a woman who knows what she wants, but she still seemed off.

"What's going on? You can tell me. It's okay."

"I won't get gagged?" She smiled.

I knew she was joking, and besides it wasn't a possibility without her consent, which she hadn't given. "Nope."

"Before I met you the most out there thing about me was that I was a lesbian. Everything else about my life was so middle-of-the-road. Everything was what I should do. Nine-to-five job. I got two weeks of vacation a year and most of that I spent on a cruise. I knew what would happen next week and next month. Only one piercing in each ear. Long hair, never dyed. No tattoos. No late nights. No drinking. No drug use. I never wore leather except for belts. I had a leather jacket, but it was a brown trench. I didn't have any butch friends. I only knew femmes. Like me. I don't even think I had any, um, you know…" She ran her finger gently along the skin on my arm. I knew what she meant.

"Black friends? What do you mean, 'I don't think'? Either you had Black friends, or you didn't." I said with a raised eyebrow.

She just nodded and sighed. "No, I didn't. Everything I knew in my heart of hearts," she said as she pressed her fist against her breastbone, "was just plain wrong and wrong for me. And I can't believe I'm saying no to you. You've been so lovely, so welcoming."

"That doesn't mean you have to do anything you don't want to. It's okay to say no to me. But don't say it to yourself. Say yes to yourself."

Her tears exploded like a flood that had been held back for years. The tears I saw when I first met Megan were from fresh wounds. These tears were old and desperate for release. I held her as she sobbed and sobbed until she was truly free.

When the tears dried up, I ordered a pizza, and we had dinner together. She usually preferred pepperoni and nothing else, but in a nod to her newly found voice and freshly discovered desires she admitted that she'd always wanted to try anchovies. I didn't care for them, so we ordered two small pizzas. She discovered she didn't like anchovies either and devoured half my veggie and sausage pizza. She kept her clothes on.

"Guess I'm learning all sorts of things." She wrapped the uneaten anchovy pizza and put it in the fridge. Kathy loved that stuff, so she could have it the next time she was here.

I nodded in agreement. "And you've so much more to learn. We all do. It never stops."

At around 10 p.m., I showed her to the guest room just down the hall from my bedroom on the second floor. She gave me a peck on the cheek. I told her to sleep well and headed into my bedroom alone.

The next morning I awoke to the sound of something sizzling on the stove. When I went downstairs Megan was there, naked once again, although still wearing my cuffs and collar. She turned to me as she flipped a sausage patty and radiated a happiness that came from deep within.

"I slept better last night than I have in years." She took a couple of slices of multigrain bread out of a bag and popped them into the toaster. We'd eaten all the bagels.

"And I do want to finish this week with you, Stevie. I want to be all yours today and tomorrow. After that, I don't know. And that's okay. But today I want to be bound to you and by you. And I want to call you Sir."

"Well, all right then."

That day we laughed. We laughed a lot.

She served me breakfast, a plate of sausage, scrambled eggs and toast. She got on her knees beside me after placing the plate in front of me. It was more than I could ask for. The sausage was peppery. She must have made it from scratch because I didn't think we had any in the house. Her breasts looked particularly beautiful today. The areolas were a rich pink, and her nipples were firm and erect.

Oh yeah, we were going to have so much fun today.

After I finished eating, she took my plate to the sink and sat down in front of her plate. Just as she was about to take her first bite I ordered her to put down her fork.

"What was your absolute favorite thing to do with me or that I did to you?"

"Being bound, Sir."

"Well, let's start now."

I got up and pulled her arms behind her, clipping her wrists to the back of her chair. This pulled her shoulders back and forced her breasts out.

She let loose a giggle, delicate like a finely wrought glass flower.

"Today you can come any time. We're just going to play. Nothing too serious."

"Yes, Sir." She might have saluted me if her hands weren't bound.

"What color are you?"

"I'm green. Very green."

Not half as green as she was a few days ago, I thought. Next, I put thin blue leather straps around her thighs. I latched them under the chair and pulled her legs as far apart as the chair would allow. The straps dug grooves into her thighs that slowly started to turn red around the edges. Finally, I hooked her ankle cuffs to loops attached the chair's legs. The set-up had the desired effect. Her breasts were completely exposed to me as was her snatch. The first few drops of wetness glistened on her pubes. Her longing glare switched from me to her nearly untouched plate of food.

I knew she was hungry. She'd get her chance to eat, but I had a few more things to do.

I grabbed an ice cube from the freezer and rubbed it down her body while I kissed her. She may not have been submitting to me completely like my other wenches, but at that moment she was totally open to me. She was submitting to me in that moment, and she was all mine. Her lips were soft, and she opened wide for my tongue. She didn't pull or struggle against the restraints. She was totally relaxed. The ice cube left drops of cold water that rolled down her breasts and landed on her wide-open thighs and made her shiver. We kissed deeply and I slid the ice cube down her flat belly. My cold fingers spread her labial lips, and she started to moan. Touching the cube to her clit elicited a gasp. Pushing it into her hole brought forth a squeal. Still, we kept kissing.

When I pulled away, she was squirming and panting. Saliva covered her mouth. Her nipples were rock hard and begging to be played with, but not yet. She needed breakfast first. Ice water dripped out of her snatch. Beautiful red marks appeared where she was bound. I asked her if she was hungry.

"Yes, Sir." Her voice was breathy.

I fed her alternating forkfuls of scrambled eggs with bits of bacon and toast. When some egg fell on her right breast, I lowered my mouth onto it and ate the morsel off her pale white skin.

"Are you ready to come?"

"Yes, but I can't," was her reply.

I knew she needed more, wanted more before she would be able to come, and I would give it to her.

I grabbed another ice cube, running it over whatever part of her skin was still dry. That cube went into her snatch as well, and her squeal this time was a little louder. I didn't have some grand plan for her, for us, today. I only knew my next move, which was to get a couple more toys from my playroom.

I returned with a pair of nipple clamps linked to a thin but sturdy chain and a vibrator with a built in special surprise for Megan. I turned it on so it would be ready when I needed it.

I started with her left tit, the one closest to her heart. I opened one of the clamps and latched it onto the flesh just behind the nipple. Attaching it directly to the nipple's tip would have caused immediate, intense pain. I wanted a slower build. This one had a combination screw and spring mechanism, but I only tightened the screw enough so that it would hang onto her tit. It would be secure enough so she would know it was there. I threaded the chain through a ring in her collar and attached the other clamp to her right tit.

The chain was loose and not taut enough for her to affect it by moving her head. That would change later.

I gave the screw on her right tit a full turn. She gasped.

"What color are you, wench?"

She gave me a big smile. Her eyes sparkled. "Green, Sir."

I gave the screw on the right tit another full turn. This time, she whimpered.

I turned my attention to the left, dragging things out even more. I slowly turned the screw eight quarter turns. At the third one, she let loose a loud gasp. By the eighth turn she was panting loudly.

"I think it's time you got some relief." My attention returned to the right nipple. I loosened it ever so slightly. Megan's panting slowed down. One full turn looser and Megan suddenly gritted her teeth as blood rushed back into the nipple. I turned the screw even more slowly until I could take the clamp off. Megan gasped.

"Thank you, Sir. I'm green."

"I'm not done yet." I gave her newly freed nipple a quick pinch. She winced.

I ran the chain back through the ring on her collar so that it and the loose nipple clamp hung down from her left nipple. I had no doubt the pressure of that extra weight made a difference. I gave the chain a yank, holding her nipple good and taut. She groaned.

"What do you want, wench?"

A bead of sweat rolled down her forehead. "I want you inside me. I want to come." Her words were punctuated with grunts and groans.

I slapped her strained left nipple. She just smiled.

I slowly loosened the screw holding the clamp on her left nipple until it let go and her tit fell to her chest. Both of her nipples were a deep dark red.

"You're almost ready."

I brought the clamp back to her right nipple. She flinched and struggled as I tightened the clamp. The second time was always more painful, more sensitive.

Once again, I ran the chain through the ring on her collar, but this time I looped it several times to shorten the chain. I reapplied the clamp to her left tit. She groaned but didn't struggle too much. The chain was so short that she had to keep her head down for any relief. The slightest movement of her head pulled on her tender nipples.

She was ready and so was the vibrator. This was one of my newer ones. It was pale pink and, most importantly for someone who has ice melting in her snatch, it was heated. It wasn't too warm, but I knew it would feel hot in her ice-cold snatch.

I knelt between her wide-open legs. Her snatch glistened with ice water and her own juices. I spread her labial lips and she let out a loud gasp.

"Oh please," she begged. "Please fuck me. Rub my clit. Let me come. Please."

The only thing I loved more than a screaming woman was one who begged.

She offered me her car. She said she would forever be my slave. She said she would never leave. People say all sorts of things under duress.

I plunged the vibrator into her hole and what came out of her mouth was incomprehensible, although I was pretty sure she was enjoying herself. I turned the knob on the base of the vibrator to give her both vibration and heat.

I think she said, "Gwaasten," but I wasn't entirely sure. She was getting louder.

I pushed the vibrator in and out while applying my thumb to her clit. Her hips bucked, pushing her snatch toward me. She was cold and warm and slippery. Her snatch smelled fresh and salty. Her thighs strained against the leather straps, and they cut deeper into her flesh. The metal rings that held her wrists and ankles to the chair started to clang as she pulled against them. And every time an orgasmic spasm made her move her head she yelped as the clamps yanked on her tits.

"You are a beautiful wench," I said. "You are a fabulous bottom. I'm so glad you know who you are now."

One last thrust into her snatch. One last yell from her and she went slack. In between whimpers she just kept saying, "Please."

I pulled out the vibrator and stood back to take a good look at her. I didn't know how much longer I would be able to see her naked, so I wanted to enjoy it. Her head hung down because of the chain attaching her tits to her neck. Her hair fell down around her face. The tendrils of her hair grazed her breasts. Sweat rolled down her forehead and landed in her eyebrows before dripping to her cheeks and then down to her lovely body. She was breathing heavily through a drowsy smile. The chain was taut. Her nipples were turning a darker red. Soon they would be released.

Her belly, which was flat when she stood, had tiny adorable rolls because she was sitting and her posture was slightly curved. I bent down to give her belly a kiss. That made her giggle.

I unsnapped the blue leather straps that bound her left thigh. I admired the marks they left behind, a row of one-inch red lines. They would fade tomorrow or the day after. But today they marked her as mine. I gently rubbed the area before letting the right thigh go as well. It was similarly marked. She winced when she tried to close her legs.

"I'm still vibrating, Sir. I can still feel you inside me."

"Excellent."

And the day wasn't over yet.

I unclipped her wrists and ankles. She flexed her arms and legs in her new freedom.

I tapped the tit clamps a couple of times. It only took the lightest pressure from my fingertips to get her to grunt and grit her teeth.

"Are you ready?"

Her beautiful smile got bigger as she clenched the arms of the chair. "As ready as I'll ever be."

With each twist of a screw, her grip on the chair got a little tighter. She grunted as blood flowed back into her strained nipples. When one clamp was loose enough to come off easily, I turned my attention to the other one. I turned that screw slowly until it too was ready to release. Megan's nipples were a little bigger and redder. I blew on them, making her giggle and squirm like she didn't know what to do with herself.

"Sir, I'm so sensitive right now."

"I know, and you're beautiful," I said.

Every day, every moment she became more beautiful. I had liked her long chestnut brown hair since the day I met her, but now I could see how charming it was when her hair fell over her deep brown eyes. Her cheekbones were high. Her skin was smooth and delicate. Even better, she could take what I could dish out and then some. Not everybody could.

She got up and tidied up the kitchen while making us some sandwiches for lunch. She kept talking about the places on her body where she could feel me. Like her nipples. Her thighs. Her snatch.

"I can feel where you kissed me on my belly."

She was so sweet.

After lunch, I hogtied her on the living room floor. She rested on her belly, reaching her hands behind her back and bending her legs at the knees. I wrapped rope around her wrists and then looped it around her ankles. She rolled back and forth on her belly, sometimes putting pressure on her still sore nipples. She would grimace and try to maintain her balance on her belly.

A hogtie was always entertaining to me because even if her nipples weren't still sensitive as all get out, there was no way for her to get comfortable.

"Are you happy?" I cinched the rope a little tighter, yanking her wrists, and thus her arms and shoulders, even closer to her ankles.

"Yep, I sure am."

I grabbed her hair, pulling her head back, and leaned down to kiss her, a big sloppy open-mouthed kiss. I removed a stray eyelash from her cheek. I ran my finger down the outside of her ear making her giggle and writhe. She couldn't get away from me, and at least right now, she didn't want to.

I ran my finger between her pulled back shoulders down her spine, and she shivered. My hand stopped just short of her glorious ass, curved and firm. I patted it gently.

"Wanna try some ass play?"

"Sure. But what does that mean? My snatch is still vibrating from this morning."

I left her struggling against her bonds and ducked into my playroom for some anal beads and a small container of room temperature lube—we'd already done enough play with hot and cold this morning. The anal beads consisted of a series of increasingly large black silicone balls connected by two-inch lengths of solid silicone. At the end was a ring to facilitate either slow or fast removal.

When I returned, she was awkwardly tilting from right to left and grunting.

"What color are you, wench?"

"I'm very green, Sir."

"Not anymore you're not."

She laughed. She had such a delicate, light laugh. I was so glad I got to hear it. I dipped my finger in the lube and started circling her puckered hole. She looked so tight. That would change. I just needed to move slowly.

She started moaning as my lubed-up finger moved around her asshole and then inside it. Her ass tightly gripped my finger. I slid gently in and out and then pulled out to get more lube. I repeated this until she was good and slippery, and my finger slid in like it belonged there. Each time I pulled out her asshole tried to close up again, but it never did so all the way.

It was time for the first bead, which was small, only a little larger than the tip of my thumb. I covered it with lube, and it slipped in easily.

With her hog tied and the anal beads hanging out of her, she looked like a strange and beautiful bug rolling back and forth on painful nipples and strained limbs.

Her moans got louder.

The second ball, just slightly larger than the first slipped in, not quite as easy as the first, but it was a comfortable fit. The third, fourth and fifth went in as well.

"How does it feel?" I jiggled the string of beads.

"Wonderful. I want more."

I couldn't say no.

The sixth bead was more of a struggle, but her smile with the seventh and eighth bead just kept getting bigger, like the beads.

"I feel so wet. So full."

"Perfect."

I sat back on the sofa and watched her struggle. Her shoulders twisted back and forth. She rolled her hands and feet. She rolled from side to side, occasionally landing on her nipples, which made her gasp. She tried to spread her legs as far as they would go, but they wouldn't go far. Eventually, she settled uncomfortably on her left side. Every so often that last anal bead would try to make an exit. I would push it back in, and she would grunt softly.

"I want all my holes filled by you, Sir." She got her request out between gasps and deep breaths.

"Well, okay then."

I went to the playroom again and came back with an inflatable gag and dildo. The dildo slid easily into her snatch. I pumped it full of air until she started to grunt. I gave it one last pump and then twisted a locking screw to make sure it stayed exactly where I wanted it, filling her hole deeply and thoroughly. Next, I inserted an inflatable butterfly gag into her mouth. This was black and looked like a soft cross. I pumped that as well until her cheeks puffed out. After I locked that as well, she returned to her fruitless struggle to get comfortable. I returned to the sofa. The gag meant that what little sound she could make was muffled. She fidgeted and squeaked. The important thing was that she was more open to me than ever. I had filled her.

I was wet and desperate for release. Yeah, my general rule was that I came first, but I was having so much fun with Megan. Sometimes rules don't matter. Sometimes you just roll with what comes.

It didn't take much stroking of my hard, bulging clit to make me come in great spasms on the sofa. Megan watched me with her happy brown eyes. I came a few times, and then sat panting.

"I'm going to be sad when you leave Megan. So sad."

She just blinked. She couldn't do much more.

I crouched down to her level. She smelled of sweat and sex, salty and musky. I reached under her and gave her nipples a quick pinch. Her squeal was muffled but high.

I turned my attention to her crotch. She spasmed every time my fingers got near her sensitive clit. She bucked when I touched it. Just when I thought she couldn't take any more I yanked on the anal beads until the lubed-up strand was in my hand. Her asshole was now open and probably would be for a while, but it was time to release her.

I let the air out of the inflatable dildo first. Her entire body was so sensitive that she flinched and spasmed at every touch. I had to hold onto her tight to prevent her from rolling away. I untied her hands and feet. She flopped flat on the rug, and then flipped over on her back to protect her nipples. I deflated the gag next, removed it and wiped the saliva off her face. She lay there for a moment, catching her breath.

I took a seat on the floor beside her and stroked her hair. I don't often say it. I don't like to admit it. I liked my short Afro-like hair, but I always secretly wanted white girl hair, especially hair like Megan's that felt so soft.

When she was ready, she sat up, too. I gave her some water and a cookie. We spent the rest of the afternoon cuddling and laughing about dates that went really badly and plans that did not go as expected. She told me about the date who showed up in dirty sweats.

"Seriously. It's a date. Put on something you wouldn't garden in."

There was the woman who wanted her to hide under a table when her ex showed up at the restaurant where they were having dinner. Megan declined but did offer to call the police. The date told her not to. There was the date where the woman invited twelve of her closest friends to join them.

Then there were the plans that went awry. She nearly missed a Caribbean cruise when her flight was late. A scholarship she was hoping for turned out to be a scam, and there was no money. Most of these stories were bittersweet, but some were downright sad.

"I was a ballerina when I was a kid. I have perfect turnout."

"I don't speak ballerina, but I assume that perfect turnout is a big deal."

"It is. I gave it up because it wasn't practical. My Dad's business collapsed when I was 11. We moved. My parents couldn't afford lessons anymore. Also, by then, I knew I was a lesbian. I wanted to be as practical and respectable as possible. I gave it up. When I realized I liked kink, I stepped up my efforts to be respectable and reliable."

I let that sadness rest in our silence for a few minutes. Finally, I said, "I would like to see you dance."

She snuggled closer to me. "I don't even know if I can do it anymore."

"It could be like riding a bike. You never forget. Or you could just take a class and find out."

She changed the subject to talk about dinner. Ballet clearly was a sore subject for her. We ordered some Chinese to be delivered. We ate while talking about tomorrow's Ace of Clubs party and gossiping about lesbian celebrities.

We didn't talk about what would happen the day after and how she didn't want to stay.

"I've really enjoyed my time with you." She kissed me goodnight and went to the guest room. I watched her walk away.

CHAPTER THIRTEEN

Megan

Today, my sixth day staying with Stevie, was fairly uneventful until we got to the Ace of Clubs. The day before had been so wonderful that I woke up feeling satisfied and safe. And I woke up alone.

I never thought I'd like that. For the past few years I'd woken up next to Paige. I usually woke up a few minutes before the alarm went off and listened to her gentle snoring. Before her I had spent about a month single after my breakup with Suzanne. Before Suzanne there had been Michelle. I had jumped from one girlfriend to the next. I had told each one that I wanted marriage, children and a white picket fence. Each one promised that they could give me that, but each one broke my heart. It was clear that I'd asked too much of them. I just wish they'd been more honest with me, like Stevie had been. I knew exactly where I stood with Stevie. I knew what she was capable of. After each break up, I slept alone, if only for a brief time, and hated it. When I left Paige, I slept on Jane's sofa bed every night feeling so small. The bed wasn't even that big, but it felt like it would swallow me whole if I wasn't careful.

Stevie seemed sad that I wasn't going to become one of her wenches, and so was I. But my heart wasn't breaking. I didn't think hers was either. I was alone in her guest room sprawled out on the cool cotton sheets that covered her queen-sized bed, but I didn't feel lonely.

I got up and made breakfast. I stayed naked and kept on the cuffs and collar. Stevie said I could take them off and wear clothes, but I didn't want to. Our relationship had already changed, but I wanted to finish the week as her wench, even if I wasn't staying. It would end, but it didn't have to end early.

I cleaned the sex toys and did some tidying up. I talked to Jane. I thanked her for her offer to come stay with her again, but Stevie had said I could use her guest room until I found a place of my own. I was going to take advantage of that offer to get back on my feet.

"Jane, I don't know what's going to happen tomorrow or next week, and I don't care. Is that weird?"

"Yeah, it is. You know me. I always have plans, goals, missions and intentions. You know what's really weird?"

"What?" I wondered what, out of all the stuff I'd told Jane recently, she would pick out as *really* weird.

"You've always been so focused and goal-oriented. All it took was one week with Stevie and you're suddenly a different person? That's really weird."

I suspect what she really wanted to say was, "That's bullshit."

"I didn't suddenly become a different person in a week with Stevie. I became the person I always was. She'd been buried under layers of respectability carefully crafted over many years. This week was about peeling those layers away."

"That sounds...painful. Oh, never mind, you like pain. Whatever."

Late that evening Kathy, April and Britney came over. I had gotten used to being naked in Stevie's house, so I didn't get dressed. I knew Kathy, of course. April and Britney were new to me. April's hair was so long and blonde, and she had the most perfect breasts. Britney's skin was a shade lighter than Stevie's. Her long, curly black hair bounced around her shoulders every time she moved. Kathy was wearing a blue rubber shift dress that was shiny and slick. April wore a long leather strapless dress held together with crisscrossed string at the sides and back that showed off her pale white skin. Britney wore a purple leather bustier that highlighted her cleavage and a black pair of snug leather pants that made her butt look great.

We were all marked as being with Stevie in some way. Kathy's dress matched the lock she always wore around her neck. April and Britney wore cuffs and collars much like mine.

We sat in the living room. They talked about how they had spent the day. Kathy had gone to several estate sales, scoring some vintage editions of classic literature. Britney had stayed in, cuddling with her girlfriend who was spending her evening with a bunch of girlfriends and going to the ballet. Misty Copeland was in town, and there was no way they were going to miss her. Britney was more interested in the Ace. April worked at the local Honda dealership and was celebrating a sale.

They were also excited about going to the Ace. The gay guys and straight folks had play parties all the time, they said, but lesbians didn't. They went out of their way to support the Ace. Only once a month, it needed everyone to show up to keep it going.

"First round is on me. Let's go. They always start off the night with demos, and I don't want to miss anything." April stood and started heading for the front door.

Britney whistled. "Big spender!"

"I sold one of the new hybrids today, so yes, I'm feeling flush," April said.

Stevie rubbed April's ass. "You're feeling flush in your wallet right now. Maybe at the Ace, I can help you feel flush in other parts."

"Oh, Stevie, you know how to turn a girl on." April laughed.

There was a lot to love about Stevie and her family. In particular, they had an amazing sense of camaraderie. They really seemed to enjoy each other's company. They seemed to be getting ready to leave, and I realized that I had absolutely nothing to wear to the Ace of Clubs that would get me there without getting arrested on the way and through the door once I got there. As comfortable as I had become with nudity, I couldn't leave the house like this, and the club had a strict dress code.

I had been enjoying not having plans, but I wasn't used to being so unprepared.

"Um....I...."

Stevie turned to me with that irresistible grin. She stuck her finger in the metal ring in my collar and pulled me up until we were nose to nose.

"Want to go out there naked?" she asked with raised eyebrows.

My shoulders dropped, but I tried to hold onto my smile. My stomach knotted. I felt safe being naked in this house even with all of Stevie's other women, but I wanted to go outside in clothes. And I didn't want to look like an interloper rather than someone who really wanted to belong to this community. Out of the corner of my eye I noticed April had a flat, white box in her left arm braced against her hip.

"No? Well, as it happens, we need to get you dressed," Stevie said. "You can get naked again at the club."

April put the box on the sofa and slid off the lid. Inside was a pile of leather with a delicate sheen. Stevie unfurled it, a long black leather dress with a square neckline, cap sleeves and a long skirt. I ran my hand over the black leather, so supple, smooth and soft.

Stevie said, "Ta-da! This is for you. Usually wenches get a permanent or semi-permanent collar after spending a week with me if it looks like we're a match, but since you're not going to stay a long time, a collar didn't really seem appropriate. I still wanted to get you something."

She kissed me and turned to April. "You know what to do."

Stevie took a seat on the sofa while the girls pulled me to standing and surrounded me. Britney put a hand on my shoulder and pushed me down to my knees. Kathy grabbed the rings on my wrist cuffs and pulled up my arms so they were reaching for the ceiling. The leather dress slid down my arms, and the world went black as it covered my face. The smell was sharp and pungent. I breathed it in deeply. The girls shimmied the dress down my torso and smoothed out the leather so that it lay flat on my belly and outlined the curves of my breasts. I had free movement, but I loved the snugness of the leather that held me like my second skin.

Kathy pulled me up to standing, and April and Britney pulled the skirt down over my hips and legs. Someone did the zipper at the back. The skirt was as tight as the bodice, and the hem landed just above my ankles. I tried to take a step toward the hallway mirror, and I stumbled into Kathy's arms.

"It's a hobble skirt, dear," I heard Stevie say. "You can't take full steps, and if you try, you'll fall. I thought you'd like it since you like bondage so much."

She had really gotten to know me. "I love it!" I said as I took a few mincing steps. That was the only way to walk without falling.

Kathy put her arm through mine and pulled me toward the mirror. I got a good look at myself and her. The cap sleeves showed off the curves of my biceps and triceps. The neckline was low enough to show an inch of cleavage. The dress highlighted all of my curves from my breasts to my waist to my calves.

"You look beautiful," said Kathy. I told her she did, too. The warm smell of my leather mixed with the odor from her rubber. I was already getting wet.

"Let's do this," I said.

They helped me down the front steps of Stevie's house and into Kathy's Subaru. I couldn't remember the last time I'd been in a car with so many people—maybe high school. I couldn't remember the last time I laughed so hard with a group of friends.

They told me more about Ace. The once-a-month club was held at a dungeon owned by a lesbian who was dedicated to keeping her space all Sapphic at least once a month. She wished she could do it more often.

When we got there, a dark noiseless side street with a large factory on one side and a couple of apartment buildings on the other, I half wondered if this was some kind of prank. Everything looked so ordinary. The grass was neatly trimmed. The factory looked closed for the night.

They helped me out of the car, and I hobbled along, gripping Stevie's arm. Her boots made a solid clomp on the concrete as we walked down a narrow gangway between two of the apartment buildings that opened out into a back area with a large coach house.

"And this, my dear Megan, is the Ace of Clubs," said Stevie.

It looked as ordinary as Stevie's home. Who knew so much lovely debauchery was hidden in plain sight and that you could only see it if you knew what you were looking at?

The shades were down, but little rays of light slipped through where the window coverings didn't quite meet the window frames. I could hear music and people moving about inside and smell the first blooms of summer poking through the dirt in a little plot to the left of the house.

April lightly slapped my leather-covered ass. "Let's get you inside."

I struggled up the half dozen front steps, and at one point the girls just hoisted me up to the entrance. The door opened to a foyer. A girl with long, straight auburn hair was perched on a stool with a clipboard. She wore a purple paisley silk corset that pushed her boobs up and cinched her waist into a perfect hourglass. On top of her pillow-like breasts rested a lock and chain far heavier than the one that Kathy wore. Kathy's could have been easily snipped. This one looked like it could foil the most determined of thieves. Stevie paid for us to get in, and the next door opened up into a wide-open combination living area and kitchen.

There was a sofa, which was occupied by a butch woman, stocky and solidly built, not unlike Stevie, except she was white. She was sprawled out, taking up as much room as possible while a feminine woman in a white leather skirt, top and stilettos curled up at her feet and ran her hands up and down the butch's legs. The butch nodded to Stevie, and then returned her attention to the woman at her feet.

The sofa looked fairly ordinary, but the long cage beside it was not. It was twice the size of Stevie's cage and waiting for its next occupant. It didn't have to wait long.

A naked gal with pierced nipples and wearing a leather dog mask was helped into the cage by an Asian woman who locked the door with metal rods that could only be removed from the outside. In response to orders, the dog-faced gal stretched out on her back on the cold metal floor of the cage. The Asian woman hooked a chain through one nipple ring, through the bars, and then through the remaining nipple ring. She did something similar with two of the rings on the dog woman's snatch. The chains were slack until the Asian woman gave them both sharp pulls, eliciting moans and squeals.

The walls were covered with rows of paddles, floggers and dildos. Even that sex shop I'd been going to didn't have this much stuff. They had every color, shape and size from a large brown dick-shaped dildo to a small pink vibrator in the shape of a bunny. The paddles ranged from small ones covered with soft red fur to large wooden ones that looked like they'd leave quite a mark.

Farther on into the club a woman was encased between black latex sheets and tormented with vibrators handled by five other women. She spasmed and screamed as best she could.

There was a cross and a spanking bench like Stevie had.

"What do you think?" Kathy asked, leaning into my ear.

"Feels like home," I said.

I surprised myself with my answer. I loved how the leather dress held my body and constricted my legs. The dress squeezed my thighs together, and my thighs squeezed my cunt, which kept getting wetter. There was no way to relieve myself without getting naked.

"I'm so glad to hear that," said Stevie who kissed me. It felt so good, loving and friendly. I guessed Kathy was playing with my hair.

And then I saw her over Stevie's shoulder.

In the center of the room was a long kitchen island. On top of it was a naked woman laid out on her back. She was covered in some places. I wasn't sure with what, but I knew who it was. It was Simone with her short curls splayed out on a small pillow propping up her head.

My friends must have noticed where my eyes had strayed to.

"Do you want some sushi? Only three dollars a piece. It's a fundraiser for the local gay youth group." April pointed at a sign near the kitchen island that mentioned the fundraiser.

"You look hungry," said Britney.

They walked me over to Simone and explained a little more. Simone winked at me as we approached. Her breasts were covered with maki rolls. Deep red tuna sushi covered her belly, although her skin showed through where someone had already taken a piece. It looked like salmon on her breastbone and eel and shrimp on her thighs. Her snatch, with matching red curls, was exposed.

We made small talk. She talked about the first time she went to the Ace, and how nervous she had been until someone handed her a flogger. Then she all of a sudden felt like she was home.

I was surprised at how comfortable I was getting with even the craziest of situations as I put three dollars in a nearby jar and plucked a maki off Simone's left breast. April had a couple of slices of tuna. Kathy went for the eel. Each piece removed revealed more of Simone's luscious skin.

I don't know how Stevie knew I wanted to be alone with Simone, but she did. With a wink, she guided her girls over to a corner with a body stretching contraption that Britney wanted to try.

I grabbed a stool and sat near Simone's head. She giggled softly every time someone removed a piece of sushi. I wondered if she was wet and if she would one day eat sushi off me. The room got quiet, and I looked over at Stevie and her girls. They had become the focus of a lot of attention.

Britney lay down on the device and stretched out her limbs. April secured Britney's ankles, and Kathy connected Britney's wrists. April and Kathy rubbed their hands over Britney's body and pinched her nipples while Stevie tightened and released a crank that pulled her limbs until she moaned and started saying that she wasn't sure how much more she could take.

"Oh, you can take more." Stevie gave the crank a half turn tighter.

Kathy lowered her mouth and bit Britney's left nipple. April's hand moved toward Britney's snatch. She let lose a short scream. The women watching them seemed turned on by the spectacle. I turned my attention back to Simone.

We became quite the team. I balanced the money jar on my lap, and women dropped their dollars in. Some looked like soccer moms from the suburbs. Others looked far funkier. A woman with a blue mohawk grabbed a piece of tuna sushi before disappearing into a corner with a woman with a shaved head behind her on a leash.

"You know, I tried that," I said to Simone. I was amazed she was so still.

"You tried what?"

"Stevie led me around on a leash, but I didn't like it. I liked nearly everything else."

I told her about my week with Stevie that was coming to a close and how I didn't know what would happen next.

"I don't know. I still don't have a job or a home. I feel like I'm on some weird pause, but I'm pretty sure I don't want to restart my old life."

"Life doesn't really stop and start. It just keeps going." She peered down at her body. "Maki's all gone. I'm flashing my boobs now." She had these pert a-cup breasts that I could probably swallow whole and a flat belly. Not a six-pack belly. It looked like it would be a comfortable place to rest my head. Maybe someday, but not today.

I told her about how I always moved too fast, and how I didn't want to do that anymore. I wanted to take some time to build the intensity.

"I like that idea," she said as someone plucked the last piece of eel sushi off her body. Now she was completely naked.

"Baby wipe time!" She sat up and grabbed the jar from me. I handed her a packet that was nearby. She wiped herself down. Her skin glowed. I sat there as she counted out the money.

"We did really well." She looked me in the eye. "And I'd like to see you again."

"I'd like that, too, but I don't want to play tonight."

Britney was on her tenth or eleventh orgasm. April and Kathy begged Stevie for a turn on the stretching table. The butch on the sofa had the woman in white leather over her knee and was giving her a good spanking. The woman in the dog mask was out of the cage but wandering on all fours behind the Asian woman. The woman with the shaved head had turned the tables on the woman with the blue mohawk and was flogging the former top on a cross.

"I know, and that's okay. When you're ready. When we're ready." Simone paused and glanced around. "This is really quite the scene. I love it."

She put her fingers in the ring of my collar and pulled me in for a kiss. We kissed deeply. I didn't pull away until I had to come up for air.

We spent the rest of the evening chatting about a new Indian restaurant that we both wanted to try, upcoming elections and the best neighborhood festivals. She talked about liking her job, and I admitted mine had been horrible.

"Maybe it's not such a bad thing that you were fired," she said.

"I think you're right."

I kissed her again and then Stevie signaled that it was time to go home. In the car, the girls teased me about Simone. I revealed that I wasn't going to stay with Stevie.

Kathy said, "That's okay. You're still a part of the family in some way."

"Every woman who spends a week with Stevie is family." Britney snuggled close to me.

That felt good. I settled into the back seat and put my head on Britney's shoulder.

I told them about needing to round up a home and a job and how I might even try a ballet class when things were more settled.

"It's been so long, but I think it's something I really want to do."

That night, April, Kathy and Britney said they looked forward to seeing me again before going home. I went to the guest room to sleep in the cuffs and collar one last time.

That morning, I slowly undid the buckles and left the leather restraints on the kitchen table next to Stevie's breakfast. I put on a T-shirt and jeans. I was no longer Stevie's wench, but I was ready to face the world. I looked in the mirror. I looked like the Megan who had arrived a week ago, but I was different. I could still feel the pressure of the leather restraints on my wrists, ankles and neck, but I felt free. Driving through the streets of a city I'd lived in for years, I saw it as if I had just arrived. There was so much I'd never seen before.

My first stop was my last home. Paige opened the door. I packed what was left of my stuff into my car. Turned out her messages about throwing out my stuff were a bluff so it was more work than I was expecting. I threw the pink sparkly high heels that I had worn on our first anniversary into the trash myself. My collection of Agatha Christie novels had never been donated to the local senior center. I would do that myself as well. I loved those books, but I had read them many times. I didn't want to carry them around anymore.

Paige put on the kettle, and I sat down for a final goodbye. She made peppermint tea.

"Do you know my favorite tea is Earl Grey?" I gave her a challenging look.

She shook her head. "I—"

"You never asked, but I should have spoken up. I should have been much more honest about how I felt."

"You're right. Maybe you should have. Maybe I should have asked." She opened the cabinet where we had kept tea. "I don't see any Earl Grey. Sorry." She sounded regretful. Her engagement ring featured a medium square-cut diamond surrounded by smaller stones. It pained me to see it, but I told her how beautiful it was.

Then she said she wanted to invite me to the wedding.

I said, "I'm going to start being more honest now. No."

I put down the nearly full cup of tea and walked out. I drove away without looking back.

By the time I got back to Stevie's house, it was mid-afternoon. I unpacked the car and put most of my stuff either in the guest room where I was sleeping or in the basement.

I had one more piece of unfinished business. I called my mother.

I told her I was fine and that, no, I had still not found a new job, girlfriend or home, although I was staying with a friend she hadn't met yet.

She said she wanted to meet my new friend, and I told her maybe. Then I said I wanted to check out a ballet class.

"I know you had to do it, but it really hurt me when I couldn't take ballet anymore. I think I want to go back."

My mother started crying. "I cried so much when your father's business went under. I know it hurt you. And I'm so glad you're going back. You know I offered it to you when things were better, but you said, no."

"Really? I don't remember that."

"Yeah, I couldn't understand why. I assumed you had just moved on. You were always really good."

That evening I had dinner with Stevie, Kathy and April at a vegan Thai restaurant. Britney was busy with her girlfriend.

Kathy picked out a spring roll from the plate a server had set down on the table. "You know, an apartment just opened up in my building."

"I'd love to see it, but I have to get a job first."

"Things don't always happen in order," Stevie said.

EPILOGUE-ONE MONTH LATER

Megan

Stevie was right. Things don't always happen in the order you want them to or think they should. I've learned that they also don't always happen as planned. Stevie said I could stay as long as I wanted, but I had stayed long enough. I took a look at the apartment in Kathy's building. It was a perfect one bedroom/one bath. Just big enough for me to live alone for a little while and move in a girlfriend when I was ready.

I didn't sign a lease right away, but while I was walking around the neighborhood just checking things out, I noticed the ballet theater was just a few blocks away. I stopped by to see if they had any classes that I could watch or even sign up for.

The classes were on a summer hiatus, but I did find out that they needed an accountant. Long story short, they hired me. The pay was comparable to my old gig without the creepy handsy lawyer. Plus, I would get free classes once they started up again in the fall. I signed the lease. I moved a couple of weeks ago and started work. And if that wasn't enough change, Simone and I started seeing each other on a regular basis.

Our first date was to that Indian restaurant we both wanted to try. In between mattar paneer and butter chicken, she told me about growing up in a small town about five hours away. She missed the wide-open skies and the neighborliness, but not the homophobia. We talked about girlfriends and dreams. She'd had a series of short-term relationships but wanted something that lasted longer. She wanted to own her own sex shop some day.

That night she kissed me goodnight, and I went home and dreamt of her.

For our second date we went to our town's annual restaurant festival and danced under the stars. We made out in my car. We had sex on our third date. We kept it pretty tame, although I was starting to feel ready for more.

I was seeing her tonight, but not just her.

I arranged a private ballet class for her, Stevie, Britney, April and Kathy. My mother was even coming. She said she always wanted to see me dance again. Jane was coming, too, and said that my life is so good that she teased me about "farting rainbows." She didn't understand my new life or friends, but, as long as we didn't tie her up, she would hang out with us.

As for Simone, I did want her to tie me up. We agreed that tonight would be our first time. My new bed had good strong bedposts. I couldn't wait.

ABOUT THE AUTHOR

Elizabeth Andre writes lesbian erotic romance, science fiction and young adult stories. She is a lesbian in an interracial same-sex marriage living in the Midwest. She hopes you enjoy her stories. She certainly loves writing them.

Other titles by Elizabeth Andre:
Lesbian Light Reads Volumes 1-6 Boxed Set (by Elizabeth Andre and Jade Astor)

Six stories of lesbians meeting the women of their dreams, having sex, falling in love and having sex again.

Each story is also available individually from Amazon, and each book can stand alone. These lesbian contemporary love stories include graphic sex and are for adults only.

Love's Perfect Vintage (Lesbian Light Reads 1)
Would you let your mother find your next girlfriend? Beautiful thirty-two-year-old African American Aisha Watson works hard all week as a budget analyst and plays hard all weekend as a competitive longsword fighter. But her heart was recently broken, and she's not even so sure she wants to be in love again after a series of dating disasters. Aisha's mother

decides to find her a nice girl and introduces her to Kris Donnelly.

Kris, with long chestnut brown hair and vibrant green eyes, is Aisha's former high school classmate who is all grown up and become one of Chicago's leading sommeliers. In between choosing fine wines, she's just getting back into dating as Aisha is leaving the scene, but Aisha is about to learn that her mother may be right about something. Could Kris be the woman for whom she's been searching?

Lesbian With Dog Seeks Same (Lesbian Light Reads 3)

Beautiful African American Jordan is quite happy spending most of her free time hanging with her dog Minnie. She doesn't need a girlfriend. Her life is just fine as it is.

Jordan's life begins to change one early Sunday morning when Minnie meets Arrow, a golden retriever, at the dog park, and Jordan meets Arrow's owner, a sexy woman with pale translucent skin and hazel eyes. Minnie likes Arrow. Jordan slowly realizes that she likes Arrow's owner even more. She has to find her again, even though she doesn't know her name, and begins to realize that her life will be even better with this woman in her life.

Bodies in Motion (Lesbian Light Reads 4)

How often does a woman get to rewrite her past and stake a claim to her future in one fell swoop?

Gorgeous Shondra Frazier gets that chance. It all starts at the "40 Under 40" reception for high achievers under the age of 40. Even though she really doesn't want the attention, she is honored because she is the first African American woman to be named manager of one of the city's top tourist attractions.

At the reception she unexpectedly reunites with her still beautiful college ex-girlfriend who broke Shondra's heart many years ago. Lynette Johnson is a former cheerleader who can still make male and female heads turn. As Lynette walks away promising to be in touch soon, Shondra spots Denyse Gabriel, one of the few African American female PhD physicists in the world and a fellow "40 Under 40" honoree. Shondra realizes attention from Denyse, with her long black hair and high collar tweed jacket, is what she wants. This beautiful scientist, however, is heading to a months-long project in Antarctica, but Lynette is sticking around and is more than willing to keep Shondra company. Shondra has to decide whether she will stay safe and start up again with her long lost college love or if she will wait for Denyse to return. Shondra can't stop thinking about Denyse, but Shondra isn't even that sure, after only one night of passion, whether the sexy physicist will want to see her when she comes back from the ice.

Right Time For Love (Lesbian Light Reads 5)

When Hannah, a 65-year-old retired nurse, goes on a Caribbean cruise with a bunch of her friends all she wants to do is win the euchre tournament. She'd like to fall in love but suspects it may be too late for her.

When Hannah recognizes an old friend from decades ago, she starts to believe that it is never too late for love. Joyce is a fellow retired nurse who lost her husband five years before and hasn't had love since. Hannah is afraid of being Joyce's vacation lesbian experiment. Joyce never thought she would find love again, and it never occurred to her that love would take the form of a woman. Together they navigate the rocky waters of love found when they both least expect it.

Landing Love (Lesbian Light Reads 6)

All Lila wants to do this winter is skate. The beautiful 20-something recreational figure skater is done with dating until mini-skirt season, at least that's what she tells her friends when she invites them to join her to visit every ice rink in Chicago.

Then one crisp morning while skating at a new rink, Lila meets Ashley. Not only is Ashley stunningly good-looking with long ash blond hair, she can land an Axel, an advanced jump that has eluded Lila. Ashley agrees to coach Lila the following weekend. When Ashley doesn't show, Lila realizes that she wasn't that serious about taking a break from dating, and she doesn't care if she ever lands an Axel. She does care about kissing Ashley but doesn't know how she will find her again.

The Beauty Queen Called Twice (Lesbian Light Reads 7)

All Lauren Golden wants is to be the best journalist ever. The gorgeous redhead with pale white skin and hazel eyes wants the story and nothing else.

When an editor tells her to interview the CEO of a successful cosmetics company, she quickly realizes she has met the woman, Charlenae White, before. When Lauren was a reporter at her university newspaper, Charlenae was a student as well and competing in the state beauty pageant. Lauren wrote about Charlenae then and never forgot her long black hair, dark brown skin and beautiful smile. After the story ran, Charlenae called Lauren to ask her out, but Lauren did not respond. Now Charlenae wants to give Lauren a second chance for love. All Lauren has to do is believe her and, most importantly, believe in herself.

Skating on Air (Lesbian Light Reads 8)

Gigi Darnell, a beautiful African American physician, has reached her early 40s with a fabulous job, a beautiful home and a bevy of nieces and nephews who love her. But being the best daughter, sister and aunt doesn't make her life complete. She wants a special woman to love who will love her back. Then she meets Lyndsey Falk, a much younger skateboarding instructor with pale white skin and eyes the color of amber. The attraction the two women feel for each other is immediate and strong. Gigi falls hard for Lyndsey, but she fears being cut off from her nieces and nephews if she makes it clear to her family that, yes, she is indeed a lesbian and not just the reliable spinster aunt, sister and daughter her family has come to expect. Lyndsey has an ex-girlfriend following her around who threatens to interfere. Together, Gigi and Lyndsey learn that skating on air and being in love will require them to be more honest with those around them than they have ever been before.

Someone Like Her (Lesbian Light Reads 9)

Nera Booker and Squeak McFadden are beautiful African American women in their early thirties, but that's where the similarities end. Nera, college educated with an upbringing in a comfortable suburb, makes a good living in health care IT systems. Squeak, with several small businesses on the go, grew up in a rough city neighborhood and has hustled for every dime she's ever made. They're madly attracted to each other from the start. Nera admires Squeak's entrepreneurial spirit, although she thinks Squeak could do even better. Squeak envies Nera's suburban childhood but wonders if maybe this accomplished woman is out of her reach. Together they learn that it's not enough to accept differences. They must embrace them if their love is to flourish.

Learning to Kiss Girls (Young adult fiction)

It's 1984, and there are lots of things the family of Helen Blumenstein, age 14, doesn't talk about. Her cousin is gay. Helen's best female friend may have a crush on her. Helen wants to learn about kissing girls, but she's scared of being different. Helen will have to find her own voice and decide if she is brave enough to be exactly who she is supposed to be, even if that means being a little bit queer.

The Time Slip Girl (Time travel lesbian romance)

What if the woman you loved was more than a century away? Dara, a computer programmer from Chicago, is visiting London when she opens a door in an Edwardian house and slips into Edwardian England. Agnes, a beautiful London shop girl, takes in the bewildered 21st century American lesbian, but, as Dara begins to accept that she is stuck in 1908, she also begins to accept that she has feelings for Agnes that go beyond gratitude. And the longer Dara stays, the harder Agnes finds it to hide her growing love for the accidental time traveler from the future. Will they overcome grief and prejudice to acknowledge their true feelings for one another? Or will Dara be snatched back to the 21st century before they can express their love?

Taijiku (Science fiction)

Angela's past is more than a little rocky, and that rocky path has led her to finish up her juvenile detention sentence on the Yemaya, an alien underwater ship devoted to observation and research. Part of its maintenance crew, at the bottom rung of the status ladder, Angela doesn't see much excitement forthcoming.

But that was before encountering the fearsome Taijiku or meeting her crew mate Stella, leaving Angela with a completely different problem and unable to say which is the greater challenge: giant sea monsters or falling in love.

Tested: Sex, love, and friendship in the shadow of HIV (LGBT fiction)

The year is 1993, and those in the gay community are dying of AIDS, caring for people with AIDS, infected with HIV or terrified of catching the virus. Edwin, Julio, Anastasia, and Jennifer are four 20-something friends who decide to spend a sunny Saturday doing the right thing: getting an HIV test at one of Chicago's public health clinics.

After, of course, they shop, have lunch, have coffee, gossip about what that person is wearing, talk about sex, lie about their sexual past, and waste as much time as they can in hopes they won't make it to the clinic before it closes for the day. They know they should get tested but don't want to.

Edwin insists that he always has safe sex with men, if he's had any sex at all, but the truth is far more complicated. Julio hardly eats, but he's so proud of his numerous sexual conquests that he gives his boyfriends both names and numbers. Anastasia's lesbian sexual history involves blood. Jennifer has boyfriends who don't always take no for an answer.

Together they learn that fear can tear people apart as much as it brings them closer, and that their blood, along with their hearts and spirits, will be tested in ways they can't even imagine.

Connect with Elizabeth Andre:

Elizabeth Andre's mailing list: http://eepurl.com/buWN8z

Elizabeth Andre's website: https://elizabethandreauthor.medium.com

Amazon Author Page: Author.to/elizabethandre

Facebook: https://www.facebook.com/pages/Elizabeth-Andre/426776437464871

Twitter: https://twitter.com/elizalesbian

Printed in Great Britain
by Amazon